P9-CBR-449

FATAL REVENGE

Other books by Phil Dunlap:

The Death of Desert Belle
Call of the Gun

FATAL REVENGE

•

Phil Dunlap

AVALON BOOKS
NEW YORK

© Copyright 2007 by Philip S. Dunlap
All rights reserved.
All the characters in the book are fictitious,
and any resemblance to actual persons,
living or dead, is purely coincidental.
Published by Thomas Bouregy & Co., Inc.
160 Madison Avenue, New York, NY 10016

Library of Congress Cataloging-in-Publication Data

Dunlap, Phil.
    Fatal revenge / Phil Dunlap.
        p.   cm.
    ISBN 978-0-8034-9861-7 (hardcover : acid-free paper)
1. Arizona—Fiction.   I. Title.

PS3604.U548F38 2007
813'.6—dc22

                                        2007016639

PRINTED IN THE UNITED STATES OF AMERICA
ON ACID-FREE PAPER
BY HADDON CRAFTSMEN, BLOOMSBURG, PENNSYLVANIA

To my wife, Judy, for her undying support. To my writers group for cheering me on, and to Sherry Crane for her excellent editorial suggestions. To the many new friends who have read my stories and graciously asked for more. And especially to the bookstores and libraries who give writers and readers a place to get acquainted.

Chapter One

They say if you're dead set on killing a man, do it in a crowded saloon, where all the witnesses are so drunk, nobody will be able to accurately identify you, or even give a hoot. That's what they say, anyway.

Two men rode slowly into the pitiful little town of Purdy as the sun dropped behind the Pedregosa range. The roar of voices in the Sure Shot Saloon became almost deafening as miners, cowboys, and storeowners alike descended on the smoky barroom intent on blowing off steam, gambling, and reveling in their few hours of freedom from grimy, back-breaking work in the blistering desert heat. In order to be heard above the din, each voice had to be a little louder than the next.

As the noise grew more intense and the drinking

1

became more serious, no one paid much attention to the two young men as they pushed open the bat wing doors and threaded their way through the boisterous crowd to the bar. They were dressed like they might be shop-keepers, nothing fancy, just neat, simple attire. Each wore a sidearm, high and slightly forward, in a manner that suggested he would be willing to use it, if such an occasion presented itself. But neither looked particular-ly interested in any sudden exchange of lead from their nickel-plated Colt .44s. They were certainly not gun-fighters, but they also didn't appear to have ever lifted a pick-ax, or wrestled a calf to the ground for branding. Both were clean-shaven except for well-trimmed mus-taches, their hands were soft, and each displayed a quiet lack of interest in the celebration going on around them.

While one of the men ordered two whiskeys, the other slowly scanned the room. His expression was hard and his gaze intense. He carefully examined the face of every man. His perusal of his surroundings stopped when he spotted one particular man in a far corner playing faro. He nudged his partner and pointed to those gathered at the table where the fast-moving card game was in full swing.

"That looks like our man," Jake said.

"Are you sure? We can't afford to make a mistake," Jed said.

"I'd bet money on it."

"You damn well better be positive, brother."

"I'm positive. That's him."

"Then let's get it over with."

The two downed their drinks then eased their way slowly across the room, taking care not to draw undue attention to themselves. They stopped a few feet from where the man playing faro grinned as he exchanged familiarities with a pasty-complexioned woman whose figure was too ample for her tight-fitting, blue gingham dress. She appeared to have stretched every seam to its limits before she began to pour out of the scooped neckline like dough rising on a stove.

The one called Jed pulled his coat back, revealing his Colt. He moved one step closer to the man they'd been watching, touched his arm and said, "Excuse me, mister, but my brother and I would like a word with you. Outside."

The man turned suddenly, with his back to the table, and with an angry growl said, "Beat it. I'm a winner here and I don't aim to have no jaspers get me off my streak."

"Won't take a minute, but it *is* important. So, if you'll do us the courtesy, we'd be obliged," said Jed.

But the man would have none of it. He spun around, his face flushed with anger. "Damn you, don't you hear good? I'm busy. Now beat it before I put a bullet in you for the bother."

Jed leaned closer and whispered something to the man.

The man's face turned red and he took a wild swing at Jed.

Jed easily sidestepped the hasty punch, then took a step back, looking at the man with hands raised as if to say he wasn't there to fight. But the other man's anger was building quickly. He hesitated only for a moment, as if he were deciding his next move, then suddenly grabbed a handful of Remington .44 and yanked it from its holster. As the man's revolver came up, Jed coolly slid his Colt from its greased holster, and in one slick, deliberate move, cocked and fired the single-action army revolver with unexpected quickness. The smoky blast blew the man across the faro table, scattering cards and money everywhere. As men fled for cover, the man with the bloom of blood on his chest breathed his last amidst a cloud of gray-white smoke and the smell of cordite.

"Let's ease on outta here before the constable decides to investigate all the ruckus, and finds that sack of garbage we left for him."

Jed slipped his Colt back into its holster, and the two of them ambled out of the saloon as if nothing more exciting had happened than a fellow spilling his drink on the floor. They mounted their horses and casually rode out of town. In minutes they were gone from Purdy, leaving one dead man and unanswered questions as to why they had sought so hard to have a conversation with that particular individual, and at that particular time.

Almost every witness said the two seemed polite, asking only that the man, a rancher named Pearson, come outside to talk. Nothing seemed out of the ordinary, and the conversation hadn't grown confrontational until Pearson got angry, apparently for no reason at all.

"One of the men seemed to be asking a question, but Pearson just exploded and drew his gun in a fit of rage," said a man who had been playing faro at the same table. Others nodded, seeming to see eye-to-eye with the man's story.

The constable wrote off the whole thing as self-defense and, after examining the body, sent for the undertaker, then returned to his small office and one-cell jail. He picked up where he had left off at hearing the commotion, mopping the floor and tidying up. No posse would be necessary tonight. The undertaker would see to it that Pearson's body was put on a wagon and hauled out to his ranch where the family could hold a wake over the next day or so, then bury him in the family plot out behind the barn.

The wooden marker would simply read: *Killed by a stranger, August 10, 1880.*

U.S. Marshal Piedmont Kelly stood for a moment, staring at the gathering dark clouds. A freshening breeze carried on it the distinct aroma of that most sought after commodity across the parched lands of the Arizona Territory—rain. *A good blow looks to be finally coming*, he thought. The streams had long ago dried up since the last gully washer roared down from the mountains. He could hardly wait for some relief from the constant blowing dust that found its way through every crack and crevice, making it almost a necessity to clean a spot on the table just to get a plate of beans to lie flat. He smiled at the thought.

He was about to enter the door to the telegraph office at Fort Huachuca when Captain Braxton, the post commander, stopped him.

"Hey, Marshal, let's go have ourselves a beer and you can tell me all about your latest exploits and how you're saving the frontier from desperadoes." Braxton cracked a smile at his own humor.

"I'd rather forget it. Don't want to bore you with tales of derring-do like those penny-dreadful novels you're always reading."

"Okay. But let's have a beer, anyway. I'm dyin' of thirst and it wouldn't be fittin' for me to be seen wettin' my whistle with any of the enlisted. C'mon, I'll buy," said the officer.

"Okay. But let me get my telegram. One of your troopers said there was one waiting here for me. I'll amble on over to your quarters in a few minutes."

Kelly knew he had little choice but to humor the captain, even though all he really wanted to do was sleep for a week. He'd been on the trail too much lately with little time in an actual bed. Rest was the most important thing to him right then.

Kelly went into the small room where the telegraph operator was hunched over the desk, listening intently to the click-clacking of the key, writing down the corresponding letters on a piece of paper. He didn't even look up as the marshal entered.

When the tapping stopped, the operator raised his chin and said, "Ah, Marshal, got that message right here for you. Sounds important." He handed Kelly a folded message and returned to straightening up a pile of small slips of paper.

Stepping from the doorway, Kelly's eyes grew wide as he read the telegram. He was still shaking his head when he knocked on the captain's door before he entered. Braxton was at his desk reading a report from a junior officer.

"Looks like someone fed you a persimmon, Kelly. Why the sour expression?"

"Do you recall an incident up on the San Pedro near Daleville a year or so ago where a man named Albert Bourbonette was murdered, and his house robbed and torched?"

"Read something about it."

"Well, there were a couple of men heading out of town who claimed they saw the men that might have done it. They described four men they saw riding away from the ranch. Gave a pretty detailed description of them, too, although it took them two days to report what they had seen."

"Oh, yeah. I seem to recall the sheriff got up a posse, but wasn't able to track down them that done it. But that was a while back. Why you chewin' on it now?" The captain took his hat from a peg and put it on.

"A man named Pearson was shot down in a saloon over in Purdy night before last. The constable had come to the conclusion that it was a case of self-defense, but as he was goin' through Pearson's things, he found a pocket watch that belonged to the murdered man from Daleville, had his name engraved on the back. And the men who confronted Pearson matched the description of the murdered man's two brothers," said Kelly.

"You thinkin' this fella Pearson was shot in revenge for something they thought he'd done over a year ago?"

"Maybe, maybe not. But I have to look into it, either way," said Kelly. "Not, however, before you buy me that beer."

The two men walked to a small, stone, civilian canteen located amongst a cluster of adobes at the edge of the post, each offering goods or services to the fort personnel at inflated prices. The canteen served rotgut whiskey and warm beer.

As they stood at the makeshift bar, Kelly took a sip of his drink. "You know," he said, "it seems strange that the Bourbonette brothers would wait so long before going after the varmints that killed their older brother. If it is them, I wonder why."

"Maybe they were out of the territory, off on some kinda business, or—"

"Or were in jail," said Kelly.

"Hmm. Yeah, that could be."

"Why'd the constable contact you? Don't they have

a sheriff over near where the Bourbonette ranch is located?"

"Good question. I wasn't involved in the search for the killers," said Kelly.

"You know anything about the situation?" asked Braxton.

"As near as I can remember, talk was that the younger brothers were more prone to going their own way than ranching. They liked fancy clothes and having the feel of spending money in their pocket."

"What are you sayin'?"

"If whoever robbed the place got everything of value out of there before burning it down, it would take a lot to start over. If the two remaining brothers had owned a stake in the land, maybe they'd figure to go elsewhere instead of building the ranch back up. I seem to remember the one named Jed was good with the pasteboards. Maybe he decided to head for the gamblin' tables."

"Makes sense. But that ain't illegal, is it?" said Braxton.

"Nope."

"What about the other brother?"

"I don't know. But I'd sure like to find out if it *was* them that confronted Pearson, and if the watch had anything to do with it."

"So, what do you aim to do about it?"

"It looks like I'm about to take a ride down to Purdy,

first, then probably head on up the San Pedro and visit the Bourbonette ranch, or what's left of it."

"What do you expect to find there besides a grave?"

"Maybe something that will tell me where the Bourbonette brothers went, or where they've been for over a year."

Chapter Two

Jed and Jake Bourbonette were in their room in the Arizona Claim Hotel in Tucson, drinking sherry from crystal glasses. Their jackets dangled from the carved wooden arms of a coat tree. The brothers lounged in shirtsleeves, their vests unbuttoned. Jake had just lit a cigar and was leaning back in a walnut armchair with a crocheted seat and back, while Jed stood at the second-floor window looking out on the street below. He held back one side of the lace curtain, silently watching each and every soul who came and went from the saloon across the street.

A slight breeze suggested the possibility of rain. Dark clouds were gathering off to the west, and the air felt moist and heavy. As the wind began to pick up, dust swirled about the hooves of every horse that trod the wide street, and women held their bonnets on with one hand while with the other they struggled to keep their long skirts from blowing up. A man's hat blew off and he chased it for nearly a block before it caught in the spokes of a parked buggy.

"Do you really think we'll find them here, little brother?" Jake asked.

"I don't know, but I'm damned sure going to keep looking. We just rid the world of one snake. Splattered him all over that faro table in Purdy. And we ain't done yet."

"What do you suppose made him go for his gun?"

"Might have been what I whispered to him." Jed chuckled.

"What'd you say? I couldn't hear a thing with all that noise in the place."

"I said I knew what he did to that man on the San Pedro a year back. Got the evidence to make him dance to the tune of the rope," said Jed.

"But we ain't got no evidence. Those varmints burned anything that might have given them up. All we got is the word of them folks that said they saw some men riding away from the ranch. And they was near a half a mile away when it happened."

"He didn't know that, now did he?" said Jed.

"S'pect not," Jake said.

Jake frowned and rubbed his chin as he pondered that.

Jed's thoughts drifted away from the conversation,

lost in wondering what his brother must have felt that evening when the sheriff broke the news to him that he'd found everything burned to the ground, after hearing about the fire at the ranch by a neighbor. Jake was told his brother's body lay crumpled in a heap on a little patch of grass under a cottonwood tree. He'd been shot, the sheriff said, and it looked like the place had been robbed of everything before it was burned.

Jed's insides churned with the sourness of revenge, and the intense desire to track down and kill every one of the four men who'd been described by others as the likely attackers. But his expectations of the excitement he'd feel when he killed one of the murderers that had wantonly stolen the life of his older brother had been disappointed. He expected to feel satisfaction, a great weight being lifted from his shoulders. So far, things weren't adding up that way. His gut ached.

Jake, too, had let his mind wander, but in a different direction as he struggled to get the expression of the man in Purdy out of his mind, that sudden recognition that swept across his face the moment he realized he was a dead man just as Jed's bullet blew him into the other life. It was vivid in Jake's memory, and it had latched onto him like a bear with a fish in his clutches, and it showed no signs of letting go. His stomach felt like he'd swallowed a dozen bees. But he was strangely emboldened with a satisfaction that went along with the queasiness.

"You *are* sure I shot the right fella, aren't you?" said Jed.

"You can count on it, brother. Just erase him from your memory. One down, three to go."

Purdy was a small town some one hundred miles across the desert, not far from a part of the Arizona Territory known to thieves and murderers as a good place to hide out. As the ground would begin to slowly rise into fields of long grass and wildflowers, the marshal would find streams lined with trees, plenty of mule deer and rabbits to hunt, and good grazing for his mount, plus a morass of switchbacks, boulder-strewn canyons, and hundreds of places for a man to hole up if he wanted to disappear, or set a trap for anyone foolish enough to seek him out. *Just like nature,* Kelly thought as he saddled his black gelding for his journey, *the most beautiful places are often the most dangerous.* So it was with an area east of Purdy called Black Skull Canyon.

Kelly had sent a telegram to the constable at Purdy, asking for information on the direction the Bourbonette brothers were last seen heading. Before leaving, he received an answer. East, the telegram had said. Due east. Kelly just shook his head.

"What's got you so befuddled, Marshal?" said Captain Braxton, who happened by as Kelly was in the middle of his head-shaking quandary.

"If the two men down in Purdy were indeed the Bourbonette brothers, they sure seem to be heading in a strange direction. They were last seen riding toward Black Skull Canyon. That's not a good place for a couple of civilized boys, if they are what witnesses figured them to be."

"Either they ain't what they seem, or they have no idea how rough that country can be for them that's unprepared for the consequences of wandering into a hell-hole of bandits and back-shooters," said Braxton. "Hell, I'm reluctant to send troops into that place."

"Well, if what the constable says is true about the shooting being a case of self-defense, and I assume it is, they aren't wanted for anything, so there's no point in my going after them."

"Well, then, what are you all saddled up for?"

"I think it's time I looked into the killing of the brother, Albert. Why was he a target for such violence? There had to be more to it than just a random murder and robbery, unless he put up a hell of a fight. Why didn't they just rob him and be done with it? Why burn everything to the ground? Sounds more like vengeance of some sort."

"A considerable number of folks out here seem prone to murder and mayhem, it happens all the time. Why bother?"

"I know, but I'd still like to know if *Albert* was the target or was just in the wrong place when the killers came by. And where were his brothers when it happened?"

"How do you expect to get answers to such questions when it happened so long ago?"

"I'll start in Purdy. I want to know how that rancher Pearson got hold of the man's pocket watch. Then, I reckon I'll head for that little town just south of the Bourbonette ranch, Daleville. Maybe somebody will remember something."

"What do you know about the circumstances surrounding this man's death?"

"Not much. As I read about it, he owned the ranch, inherited when their father died. His brothers weren't much interested in getting their hands dirty. Albert was said to be a tough, crusty rancher, and not all that easy to work for. Anyone hired as a ranch hand could forget trying to get away with sloughing off. A newspaper obituary said he was 'tough as nails, and twice as driven.' I was never quite sure what that meant. I do know he had trouble keeping decent help."

"So you never went up there to look things over?" said Braxton.

"The sheriff at the time seemed competent to do his job. I sent a telegram asking if he needed help. He sent back that he had it under control. That's the last I heard of it. Until now, of course."

"Pretty much a local matter, anyway, I reckon."

"Yep. But now it looks as if I'd better at least sniff out the edges of the situation, especially if these brothers have decided to start a war of revenge."

Jed was anxious to leave the hotel room and get on with the search for their brother's killers.

"That was a smart idea you had of heading east, then doubling back for Tucson just to throw off anyone that might be interested in our whereabouts. Let's take a walk through some of the saloons here," said Jed. "Maybe we'll scare us up a murderer or two."

"We don't even know if they headed this way. Why, that fellow you gunned down was near a hundred miles southeast of here. What makes you think the others'd come here?" Jake asked.

"Won't know till we look around, now will we?" said Jed.

Jake sighed and lifted out of the chair he'd been buried in for nearly two hours, trying to sort out his feelings about the whole situation. After all, he wasn't *really* a killer. He was a businessman, the proprietor of a small dry goods store in Daleville. He'd never faced a man bent on killing him in his life. His brother Jed, on the other hand, had claimed to have gunned down five men in his lifetime, although Jake had never been anywhere near when the shootings were supposed to have occurred.

Jed had spent the past year down in Louisiana, working the riverboats, while Jake stayed in Daleville, taking care of business, and trying to build up enough cash to get into mining, something for which he'd always had a fascination. The dry goods business had been less successful than Jake had hoped for. Cash was always in short supply. He and Jed had not seen each other for over a year. Fact was, Jed claimed to have been unaware of Albert's murder until returning to Daleville just recently.

And as Jake seemed lost in his own thoughts, Jed, too, was pensive. He had found himself in the middle of something he wasn't certain he wanted to be involved in. Sure, he wanted to see justice done, but at what cost? By shooting the man in Purdy, he'd already traveled down the road to the fatal revenge he knew in his heart was what he owed his brother. The day Jake told him about Albert's death he was heartsick and so angry he could have killed the first person he saw, guilty or not. But a few weeks had put some distance between him and that anger, and time offered an opportunity for questions to crop up. Questions that had him wondering not only who would do such an evil thing, but why? He had to admit the thought had entered his mind that Albert's unyielding stubbornness might somehow have gotten him killed. The three brothers had certainly had their differences over the years, starting with his and his brother Jake's refusal to stick around to help with the ranch after their parents had died. Of course, he quickly squashed those thoughts, but they lingered, nevertheless, in the far reaches of his imagination.

"Jake, I'm counting on you to carry your weight in tracking those vultures down and paying them back for their treachery," said Jed.

Jake nodded. "All right, Jed, I'll be right there with you, but we gotta be careful. I don't intend to get myself hanged for killing some innocent man."

"There's no such thing. Every man's done something

he should hang for. Just means he never got caught, that's all."

"Have you ever committed a hanging offense, Jed?"

Jed looked away from his brother, walked to the window, and parted the curtain. He stared at the street for several seconds before answering.

"What difference does it make? I'm not wanted for anything. Let's just forget all this nonsense about hangings. We got ourselves a mission, and we have to keep our minds on that. Our brother is lying dead in the ground, murdered for no good reason. He was blamed ornery at times, but he didn't deserve what happened to him. The law didn't catch them that did it, so now it's up to us to make things right."

"Who did you kill, Jed? I need to know."

Jed pushed past his brother, grabbed his Colt and holster off the table, strapped it on, and opened the door. He was halfway down the stairs when he heard the door slam behind him and footsteps coming down the stairs. He smiled to himself as he walked through the lobby of the hotel, mindful of his brother following closely.

Chapter Three

Riding most of the night to avoid the mid-day heat, Marshal Kelly arrived in Purdy mid-morning. He stopped first at a small boarding house on the edge of town to inquire as to the availability of a room for a couple of nights. He found a smallish woman, dressed in denims and an oversize rough cotton shirt with the sleeves rolled up, scrubbing down the front porch in preparation for a much-needed whitewashing. Blowing sands had nearly obliterated the paint in spots and mud splattered the first two feet of the wood siding all around, the result of heavy downpours during the monsoons.

He dismounted and tied the gelding to a hitching post in front of the house. He stopped short of clomping onto the newly swept and scrubbed floor; he wouldn't enter without an invitation.

"Ma'am, I'd like a room if you have one available," he called to her.

She stopped working, walked to the edge of the porch and squinted at him, her round face lined with the gathering history and hard edges of frontier life.

"Name's Maggie. You wanted for anything, mister? I don't abide rustlers or robbers in my house. I also won't have you stompin' dirt all over my carpets, neither."

"No, ma'am, I'm not wanted for anything. And I'll do my best to stay clear of mud puddles."

"Well, all right, you look like a reasonable sort. C'mon in and I'll show you to your room. If you like it, it's four bits a night. You can stable your horse out back."

She hurried inside with Kelly right behind her. She stopped at a room near the rear of the house. It was clean, though sparsely furnished. One window looked out over a small corral made of dried ocotillo spires held together with strands of wire. The place seemed quiet and that was its most appealing attribute after his long ride.

"Looks fine. Do you serve up a meal?"

"Breakfast and supper, included in the price. Be here on time, and you can eat your fill. Be late, and you get whatever's leftover. Got some other boarders, so you got competition for the tub if you want a bath. That's ten cents extra," she said with a wink. "But if you was to take my advice, first one to the tub gets the clean water."

She chuckled all the way back down the hall as Kelly went back out to unsaddle his horse and get him some grain. That done, he came back in and leaned his Winchester carbine against a chair, took off his gun belt and hat, and dropped onto the bed. He pulled off his boots, and fell back onto the thick feather mattress. With a sigh of comfort, he was asleep in minutes.

Kelly awoke late in the afternoon to the smells of freshly baked bread wafting through the house. He dressed and followed his nose to a dining room where four other people were already seated. The long table was filled with bowls of beans, baking-powder biscuits, and peaches fresh out of the can. He took an empty chair just as the lady came through a curtained doorway with a platter of meat.

"Well, mister, I see you got yourself up just in time."

"The smell of cooking acts as a natural alarm clock," he said. The others chuckled.

One of the men seated at the table asked Kelly what he was in town for. Kelly took his time telling his purpose as he was almost ravenously devouring a tender piece of beef. After a minute, he sat back, wiped his mouth and droopy mustache, and looked around the table at the others. All of them looked like average, weather-beaten cowboys except one, a well-dressed, clean-shaven older man who appeared to be one who might be well versed in the town's doings. It was this man who had inquired of Kelly's reason for being in Purdy.

"Well, sir, I'm here to see about the man that was killed here last week."

"The fella who got shot at the faro table over at the Sure Shot?"

"That's the one. Know anything about him, Mister, uh—?"

"Seth Bonner. I own the mercantile. What's your interest in Pearson?"

Kelly pulled aside his vest, revealing the silver marshal's badge.

"Oh, a lawman, huh? Well mister, what if I was to tell you that skunk had it comin' to him?" said Bonner.

"I'd say I heard it was self-defense, but that I still needed to look into it. Now, do you know anything useful, or not?" Kelly's eyes narrowed as he watched everyone at the table for changes in their expressions. He saw nothing but a bunch of hungry cowboys who appeared to care little for whatever had befallen Mr. Pearson. The expression on the face of the man asking the questions was another thing altogether.

"I was there when it happened. Yeah, I'd have to say it was self-defense on the part of the fella done the shootin'. But I can't say them two dandies that came up to Gold didn't have it in mind to gun him," said Bonner.

"Gold?" asked Kelly, with a quizzical look.

"Gold Pearson. That's the man that was shot. His momma named him and his twin brother after the strikes that occurred in the area just before they was born."

"So, this Gold Pearson had a brother?"

"Yep. Silver Pearson, the twin brother. Can't tell them two apart for love nor money, and that's the truth," said Bonner.

"Have you known the Pearsons long, Mister Bonner?" said Kelly.

" 'Bout ten years, ever since I built my store across the street."

"What can you tell me about them?"

"Hard men to get along with. Gold was tough as month old beef, a soul with a quick temper and an unforgiving nature. A mite contrary for my taste. A natural born gambler. Silver, on the other hand, is just a no-good, worthless loafer. Never did a lick of work in his life. Drifts in and out of town like a tumbleweed in a stiff wind. And he takes too much pride in showin' off his familiarity with that Remington he totes with him everywhere he goes."

"The two men that rode in, maybe looking for Pearson, did you know them?"

"Never laid eyes on them before. But it was clear Pearson was the reason they were here. They weren't in town but a short time," said Bonner.

"Sounds like I need to have a talk with this Silver Pearson," Kelly said, returning to some serious eating.

The other three men at the table quickly finished off their dinners, excused themselves, and made a hasty exit. Outside, they stood by their horses for several minutes, locked in a seemingly serious discussion. Kelly could see through the window that they appeared to be having different opinions about something. They kept their voices low so as not to be overheard. Finally, they mounted up and whipped their horses to a run, heading straight out of town, as if on some mission of considerable importance. Kelly found himself wondering whether it had to do with Gold Pearson's death. The only way to find out was to go to the Pearson ranch, a trip he intended to make early the next morning.

But there was another person he needed to consult first—Constable John Zachary Jackson. As soon as Kelly finished his meal, he got up, thanked Maggie for cooking up such fine victuals, and strolled outside, looking first one way then another in an attempt to identify the constable's office. He didn't have to look far, as the town had but one street. A small, crooked sign hung out over the entrance of the inauspicious domain of an unkempt and overweight man wearing a floppy hat and wide suspenders that curved around his stout belly like splayed railroad tracks.

"Constable Jackson?"

"That's me. State your business, Mister, or keep on movin'. I got no time to palaver."

"U.S. Marshal Piedmont Kelly. I'd like to talk to you about the shooting of Gold Pearson."

"Ahh. You're the one I sent the telegraph message to. Well, there ain't a whole lot to tell, Marshal. It was a clear case of him pullin' his hogleg first, but bein' a mite slow on the trigger. Didn't see any reason to go after them that shot him, so I figured to let them move on before any trouble started, and they did."

"You said in your telegram that you'd found a pocket watch on Pearson that belonged to a man who died a year back near Daleville. Do you still have that watch?"

Jackson groaned as he pushed himself out of the captain's chair that he'd leaned back against the outside wall of the adobe jail. He shuffled inside, motioning Kelly to follow. The old constable was a sorry sight, and it was obvious he wasn't getting wealthy as the law in Purdy. The seat of Jackson's pants were threadbare, and the seams were stretched almost to the breaking point. His gun belt hung below his bulging stomach with his holster and converted Remington skewed towards the front. The constable sat heavily in a rickety swivel chair behind his desk. He opened a drawer and pulled out the watch and gold chain. He dropped them on the desk.

"That's what I found in his pocket. See there, on the back, it's engraved with that man's name. I remember reading about him getting shot and his place burned 'bout a year back. Couldn't get it out of my mind, so I remembered his name. What do you figure it means, Marshal?"

"At this point, I'd have to guess it all adds up to a

case of vengeance. But it's a mite early to be making such suppositions. The two that confronted Pearson fit the description of the dead man's brothers, Jed and Jake Bourbonette."

"You figure they tracked Pearson down thinkin' he had somethin' to do with the shootin'?"

"That's what I aim to find out. Got any idea where Pearson was about the time the man was shot?"

"That's a long time back, too long for this old head to wrap around any rememberin'. I will say I can't imagine Gold Pearson doin' such a thing. He was mean, but I never figured him for a killer. Why'd he go off and do a thing like that, takin' a chance on getting' killed himself?" Jackson cocked his head to one side and looked at the marshal without raising his head, as if to suggest he was leery of any such notion.

"Right now, I can't answer those questions. I understand Gold had a twin brother. What's he like?"

"Silver? Worthless, no-good jackleg. See him about four times a year when he comes in town to get a snootful of whiskey. He gets good and liquored up, shoots up the town, and then off he goes to who knows where, raising a ruckus and causin' someone else misery."

"Can you think of any reason why Gold was in possession of this watch?"

"It's a mystery to me, Marshal. Might ask out at the ranch, although, you may find Pearson's brother a mite touchy about the whole incident. I'd seriously consider stoppin' at the gate first and callin' out to let him know who you are. Otherwise, you might be pickin' double-ought buckshot outta your hide." Jackson grinned at the picture he'd just painted.

"I'll be real careful, Constable. Thanks for your help." Kelly left the constable's office and wandered into the Sure Shot Saloon where Pearson had been plugged, hoping to find someone who was there the night of the shooting. There were surprisingly few patrons at that time of day. He walked up to the bar and asked for a beer. The bartender drew one and set it in front of him. The overflowing foam melted down the sides of the glass to form a puddle.

"Bartender, were you here the night Pearson got killed?"

The bartender was a skinny man with slow eyes and a turned-down mustache. His thinning hair was combed over and greased down like dark strings.

"Uh-huh. Why'd you want to know?"

Kelly let the man see his badge.

"Kinda late, aren't you? He's been in the ground for a week now. Besides, what's to know? He was slow on the draw, and that usually gets you just what he got—dead."

The bartender moved Kelly's glass over to allow him to mop up the spill, then leaned back against the back-bar, hooking his thumbs in his apron ties.

"Did you hear either of the two men that were involved in the fracas mention Pearson by name, or say anything about him before the shooting took place?" Kelly said.

"Nope. You ought to be in here at night and try to hear anything with all them cowboys trying to shout one another down. Besides, we got ourselves a piano player who was poundin' them ivories pretty good just before the shot rang out. All I remember was they ordered a whiskey, paid for it, then wandered over to the faro table. That's when Pearson got itchy about somethin' and one of them boys ended his itch. That's about all I know."

Chapter Four

Jed and Jake Bourbonette took seats at a table at the far side of the saloon, away from what little activity there was in the middle of the day. Only a few men were scattered about the room, three were leaning on the bar, and card players occupied two of the tables. A gambler seemed to be sizing up his prospects of winning enough hands of poker to send three potential suckers packing with little more than drink money between them. After several minutes, one of the cowboys turned and left, shaking his head. The other two must have felt their chances were good enough to come out winners, as they both sat down at the gambler's table. The gambler pulled out a deck of cards and slapped it down in front of them, then tapped the cards. One of the two cut the deck, and tossed a bill in the center of the table. His friend did the same. The gambler added his dollar and began dealing.

Jed looked at Jake and grunted, "That game won't last long. Those two fools will be broke before lunch. Keep an eye on the dealer's hands. He's not very good, but he's better than those two."

"Some folks just never seem to learn when they're better off walking away," said Jake.

The brothers watched the game progress for a few minutes, taking note of how consistently the hands seemed to favor the gambler, and how the cowboys hadn't caught on, even as their meager stacks began to dwindle.

"I see the way you're lookin' at that pasteboard pirate, Jed. Are you thinking about sittin' in and cleaning him out yourself?" Jake was shaking his head.

"He's pretty pitiful. It might be a good lesson for him. I could have him crawling out of here in no time with nothing but the shirt on his back."

"I think I'll go back to the room, then. I'm not interested in taking any chances with what little money I'm carrying. Since you're the gambler in the family, you go ahead, if you think you can take him. We could use a better stake if we're going to keep up the hunt for them killers," Jake said. With that, he got up and left his brother leaning back in his chair, sipping his beer, and grinning from ear to ear.

"Silver! When we were in at Maggie's, we overheard a marshal in town talkin'. Says he's fixin' to come out here and palaver with you about Gold's gettin' shot," said Daniel Free, one of the cowboys from the boardinghouse in Purdy after he'd returned to the Pearson ranch.

"What'd he say?"

"Well, we was all eatin' and he was jawin' with Mr. Bonner, and the subject of you and Gold come up, and the lawman asked what you two was like, and—"

"Get to the point, Daniel. I ain't got all day. What'd Bonner say about it?"

"Bonner just said from what he'd heard, it appeared them two that rode in had come lookin' for Mr. Gold. Sorta like they was gunnin' for him in particular."

"Yeah? What'd he have to say about me?"

"Not much."

"Exactly how 'not much?'"

"He said you was ... uh . . worthless and, uh . . . lazy."

Silver grabbed the brim of his hat and swung it into Daniel's face, knocking him back a step. Daniel frowned as he straightened his own ratty, well-worn, and sweat-stained old bowler.

"I, I didn't mean nothin' by it, just tellin' you what the man said. Just like you asked."

Silver stormed off towards the bunkhouse. He yelled for the foreman, Galt, to round up any of the hands that were scattered around the ranch to come in for a meeting. Galt went on a run for his horse. He mounted up and kicked the bay mare to a dusty run toward the nearby hills. Almost all the hands were close-by—all, that is, with the exception of four of them that were out repairing some fencing around a distant water hole. They, too, would be expected at the meeting. When he finally saw them, he stopped short at the top of a ridge and fired his revolver twice in the air. He called out for them to hightail it back to the bunkhouse, pronto. After making certain they had heard him, he swung his horse around and headed back, himself, in a cloud of dust.

As Galt and the others came straggling in the bunk-house door, they saw all of the other hands gathered around, some standing, some squatting, as Silver Pearson stared angrily at the floor, his thumbs hooked in his gun belt.

"'Bout time the rest of you got here. What I've gathered you together for is we may have ourselves a problem. There's a lawman in town who says he plans to come on out for a visit. Wants to talk about Gold's killin'. Now, men, if he gets too curious, we may have to deal with him harshly, if you catch my meanin'."

"What do you want us to do with him, Silver?" Galt said, as the others looked to each other with expressions that ranged from quizzical to some sort of evil anticipation.

"We'll first listen to what he has to say. If it don't sound right, we might just have to make sure he don't get back to town with it. If he's just askin' some questions to kinda lay the whole thing to rest, well, maybe

I'll feel generous and let him live," Silver said to a roar of laughter.

"What if he starts proddin' one of us about what we might know about some of the ranches that have been robbed the last couple of years?" said Galt.

"Shut up, you damned fool!" Silver quickly glanced around at the others, in particular the newest hires who likely would have had no idea what Galt was even talking about. Several of the men confirmed Silver's outburst by looking at each other with questioning glances. A dark frown came across the face of one young cowboy who had been with the outfit less than a month. He said nothing, but was visibly shaken by Galt's question.

"Don't listen to that idiot, men. He's talkin' about somethin' that ain't none of us got nothing to do with. Just you never mind his loose mouth. Sometimes he gets it up and runnin' before his head can see it comin'," Silver said.

The men all laughed. Galt looked sheepish.

Kelly asked directions to the Pearson ranch from Maggie. She was showing signs of getting ready to tackle whitewashing the front of her house. She had lined up a couple of buckets, three brushes, and some old rags, presumably to wipe up any mistakes.

"You ride straight east for about three miles, Marshal, then take a right where the road sorta splits. You go another four or five miles, and there it is. It's a dingy, run-down place with a few scrubby cattle and a barn that could fall apart of its own accord in a stiff breeze. Why'd you want to go out there for, anyway?" She put her hands on her hips as a mother would when scolding her child.

"I need to ask a few questions of the one called Silver. His brother getting himself shot has brought some things to light, and I reckon you could say I just need to get a feel for where those folks stand," he said.

"Well, you might as well know, the citizens of Purdy don't have much to do with them in general. Some of them cowboys drop in for breakfast or supper once in a while if they got business in town, but they don't mix with the locals."

"Is there bad blood between the town and the Pearsons?"

"Can't say it's exactly bad blood, but most folks feel a powerful sense of discomfort from the whole Pearson bunch. There's somethin' not right out at that ranch."

"What is it that has everybody so concerned?"

"It's mostly a question of how they survive. They got no herd to speak of. They raise no crops. They don't hold down no jobs in town, nor anywhere else near as we can figure."

"But they still have plenty of money. Is that what you're trying to say, Maggie?"

"That's exactly what I'm sayin', Marshal. And that makes the rest of us a mite edgy. Sounds more like a gang that goes off, robs folks, then comes back to hide out under the guise of legitimate ranch owners. I know, don't bother to say it, we ain't got no proof of any of it. And you're right."

Kelly rubbed his chin for a moment, then thanked Maggie for the directions. He mounted his black gelding and slowly rode out, taking heed of Maggie's admonition to be careful. The road east was generally flat and wide, but it narrowed as he approached the turn-off to the Pearson place. As he neared the ranch boundary, he noticed how the road showed no signs of wagon tracks, as most working ranches would. Only horses coming and going. And not too many of them, either.

When Kelly arrived at the front gate, he noticed a crude wooden arch above the rickety gate that said PEARSON RANCH. PRIVATE. Kelly reached down and pulled the latch, letting the gate swing freely. He rode through, then continued on down the trail to what he hoped would be a ranch house. He rounded a curve between two hillocks that were covered with boulders and beyond he saw a cabin made of stone with a porch made of crude timbers and a shake shingle roof.

The cabin itself looked sturdy enough, but it was clear there was little regular maintenance done to keep it from going the way of all things man-made in the desert. Two windows, grimy from blowing dust, looked as if they'd never been washed, so trying to catch a glimpse of what might lay beyond the panes was futile.

As he glanced around, it was clear Maggie had been right: it *would* make a perfect hideout.

He dismounted and called out to anyone who might hear.

"Hello, the house. Is anyone here?"

A man appeared from around the side of the building. He was tall and bulky, wearing denims and a blue shirt. His hat was pulled low over his eyes and he carried a Remington .45 at his side. His boots were dusty, but not beat-up. From the scowl on his face, his manner was certain to be confrontational.

"What do you want? Didn't you see the sign? It said 'Private.' Can't you read?"

"I'm a U.S. marshal, and I'm here on official business. And I don't need an invitation. You Silver Pearson?" Kelly said in the same tone as the greeting he'd received.

"Yeah. I'm Silver. State your business and do it quick. I'm busy. This here's a working ranch. Precious little time to jaw with the law."

"I didn't see much activity as I rode in. Where are all your hands?" Kelly said.

"They're around, if it's any of your business. Now what is it you wanted?"

"I'd like to ask you about a gold watch that was found in your brother's pocket. It was engraved with the name of a man who was murdered about a year back up near Daleville. What do you know about that?"

"Why, er, nothing. I didn't know he had anything like that. Probably some cheap timepiece he bought from a drummer, or he may have found it somewhere and just picked it up and slipped it into his pocket. I 'spect he forgot about it himself. Couldn't have been important or I'd have known about it."

"So, you never saw the watch?"

"No. Why would he show it to me? Now, was there something else?"

"Is there any chance Gold was up along the San Pedro about this time last year?"

"Nope. He was right here with me. We was gettin' ready to take some cattle over to Fort Bowie."

"Where are your womenfolk? I don't see any signs of the feminine touch."

"Our ma died a few years back. Ain't none of us married. What's that got to do with this watch, anyway?"

"Usually, when a man carries a watch in his pocket, he takes it out now and again to tell time by. Maybe Gold had a reason to keep it a secret."

"Gold didn't have no time for secrets. Like I said, this here's a workin' ranch. Now, if you don't mind, I'll just get back to doin' what I was before you come ridin' in, uninvited."

Silver turned abruptly and stalked away, leaving Kelly standing all alone. The marshal climbed into the saddle, and heeled his gelding around. He paid particular attention to several ranch hands milling around the bunkhouse. *If this place has so damn much work need-*

ing done, why are those fellas just loafing around? he thought. He urged the gelding to a trot as he surveyed the land around him, land that was showing little attention, and no sign of any livestock.

As he reached the pass between the two hills, he caught sight of something shiny up in the rocks. Without thinking about his actions, he dove from his saddle just as a bullet sang by his ear, ricocheting off a nearby boulder.

Chapter Five

As far as cleaning out the gambler in a hurry, Jed's luck seemed to have taken a turn for the worse. He had taken only four of the past twenty hands, and his poke was getting thinner by the minute. He was about ready to throw in the towel, when he noticed a tiny corner of what looked suspiciously like a playing card poking out from the gambler's sleeve. *Damn*, he thought, *this tinhorn has been palming the pasteboards.* He quickly changed his mind about quitting and set out to teach the man a lesson. One he would never forget, assuming he survived, of course.

"Let's get ourselves a new deck, pardner. This one's gettin' frayed about the edges," said Jed. He stood up, straightened his waistcoat, rolled up his sleeves one turn, adjusted his gun belt, and sat back down. He called out to the bartender to bring over another deck. His thin face reflected an air of renewed seriousness.

The gambler nodded his acceptance of Jed's request, but his complexion took on a definite pallor. He began to squirm in his chair as if his lace-up shoes were too tight. Perspiration began to bead up on his brow and he kept clearing his throat.

"Something bothering you?" said Jed, as the bartender tossed the new card deck onto the middle of the table.

"No, no. It's just that I'm growing tired. I may have to drop out of the game for awhile."

Jed ignored the man's blatant attempt to resign the game and get away scot-free with the money he'd already cheated several players out of. Jed broke the deck and began to shuffle them. He laid the new cards in front of the gambler and said, "Your cut."

Nervously, the gambler tugged at his collar and in a hoarse voice said, "You know, I think I'll be leaving you. Maybe you can get up a game with some of the new cowpokes that are gathering at the bar. I'd bet they're eager to mingle with some fresh blood."

The gambler started to get up.

Jed leaned over and in a voice barely above a whisper said, "Mister, if you don't stay rooted to that chair, the only way you're going to leave this saloon is feet first. I have a .45 in my hand beneath the table and if you don't play one more hand, just to prove you haven't been cheating, I'll pull the trigger. I can easily explode your heart before you can even find your Remington. Now deal."

The gambler dealt. With each card, Jed raised the pot, until he was all in. The gambler was forced to meet him at every turn. Jed kept a keen eye on the tip of white card that stuck ever so slightly from the gambler's boiled and starched sleeve.

"Well, will you look at that. My luck seems to have turned around," Jed said as he spread three aces and a pair of sixes out in front of him. The gambler tossed his losing hand on the stack of money in the pot.

"I, uh, really do have to be going, now," mumbled the gambler.

"Why, you've still got a few dollars left there. Let's just have one more hand so I can see if I can take it all. Don't that seem reasonable to you?"

"Why would you want to see me broke down to my last nickel?"

Jed leaned across the table and said in a low whisper, "Because of that card that is stickin' outta your sleeve. You're a downright rotten, snivelin' snake. If you try to walk out of here with so much as one dime, I'll blast your cheatin' head clean off."

The shaken man smiled a defeated smile and nodded. Perspiration now ran down his forehead like a waterfall.

Jed took the last hand, and the rest of the gambler's money, with a pair of jacks. He gathered his winnings into his hat, got up from the table and sauntered out as the gambler leaned back with a relieved sigh as if he were thankful to have escaped with his life after getting caught cheating.

"It's been a pleasure, sir," Jed called back as he pushed through the door.

When Jed entered the hotel room, he found Jake asleep in an overstuffed, wingback chair pulled up near the open window. A light breeze was wafting the curtains, and the room was fragrant from a handful of fresh-picked flowers in a jar that sat on the table. Jake awoke when Jed slammed the door behind him. He flew into the room and emptied his hatful of money in the middle of a table, then silently counted it before scraping it off into his coat pocket.

"What'd I tell you, brother? Didn't I say I could take that miserable pasteboard pusher? And here it all is, every penny he had to his name."

"You really did it, and still managed to get out of there with your skin intact? Hmmm, good fortune seems to have overcome you."

"Why, whatever do you mean, brother? It's simply a matter of skill, not fortune."

"Uh-huh, and some fancy slight of hand, I'll venture. Where'd you learn all them tricks purveyed so handily by those 'genteel loafers?' "

"You want to know where I've been for the past ten months? Well, I spent some time learning the tricks of the trade from the best carders in the business. I been on the Mississippi and the Missouri, on paddle-wheelers, and let me tell you, that was some experience."

"Yeah? Then how come you showed up here broker than an old spoke?"

"I ran into a string of bad luck over in El Paso. And that's all I'm goin' to say about it. But I'm on my way to reclaiming the losses, don't you worry none," said Jed. He walked over to the table and picked up a decanter of sherry and poured some into a glass. He downed it all in a single gulp.

"I thought we were here to find ourselves some killers, not to skin the locals. If this is nothing more than a gambling lark for you, then I'll take my leave and head on back to Daleville. My enterprise is sure to need my attention," Jake said.

"Oh, don't go gettin' so damn pure and innocent on me. You've done your share of less-than-legal deeds, or would you rather I didn't bring those up?" said Jed.

Jake looked away, reached over, and drew the curtain open with the back of his hand. He gazed down on a street bustling with wagons, buggies, and citizens hurrying about their business with no knowledge of the two strangers on the second floor, scanning every face for their next victim. He was growing anxious to get on with the search for their brother's killer, but just as eager to return to Daleville to resume his life and put all this behind him.

In a strange way, he envied Jed for his seeming lack of concern over what could happen to them if they identified an innocent man for their fatal vengeance, and ended up on the wrong end of a rope. Jed's cavalier attitude seemed out of place for such serious business, and yet there was a certain appeal that surrounded his brother, a natural charisma that made Jake envy his style. But then, Jed *was* the youngest, and he'd been a wild hare from the start.

Kelly was drawing fire from more than one rifle. They had him pinned down behind a boulder with no chance to get to his horse and retrieve his Winchester. *At this distance, a sidearm is of damned little use,* he thought. He was in a tight spot. He could identify at least two shooters, possibly as many as three, each of whom was at least seventy-five yards away, bunched together, and well-hidden up high in the rocks.

Kelly's horse had shied away several yards, far enough that getting to him to retrieve his own rifle would be a long shot at best. He didn't want to whistle the gelding nearer for fear of the horse taking a bullet and leaving him afoot. He could probably throw some lead from his Colt in the direction of his attackers, but whether it would be enough to make them keep their heads down long enough for him to make it to the rifle was a toss-up. So, for the time being, he would stay put, and hope the cards would begin to fall his way.

Besides the bullets whizzing by his position, he was damned uncomfortable jammed up against the boulder, half-sitting, half-lying on the rocky ground scattered with sharp stones and the needles of long dead cacti. He was getting thirsty from being directly exposed to the blazing sun. And his canteen was tightly wrapped around the saddle horn. As near as he could figure, those cowboys had sent about fifty shots his way with no sign of letting up. He knew he couldn't rush them because they were far enough away that his shots would be ineffective until he got to within twenty-five yards or so. But those rifles were accurate well past one hundred yards. Fortunately, there was nothing but scrub past where he huddled for the shooters to hide behind or they would surely have begun circling around him to squeeze him in a crossfire. That would pretty much put an end to the day's shooting competition, and to him. Of that he had no doubt.

What he couldn't figure was the why of it. All he'd done was ask a few questions of Silver Pearson that really had nothing to do with him or any of his men. He'd made no accusations. Why take such offense to his questions, not to mention take the risks involved with trying to gun down a U.S. marshal? His thoughts turned to the pocket watch that had been found on Gold Pearson's body. That might have been the catalyst to his being jumped. If so, there was much more to the story, and it was now taking on more significant proportions.

Since Kelly had yet to return one single shot, he figured his ambushers would soon either have to get more ammunition or come down to find out why he hadn't thrown any lead their way. Let those fools up in the rocks make all the moves and he'd see what transpired. He leaned back and tugged a bag of tobacco from his shirt pocket, then pulled a sheath of papers out to roll himself a quirly. When he had sufficient tobacco on the paper, he rolled it, licked one side, stuck it in his mouth, and struck a match on the boulder. *Maybe the sight of smoke coming from my position might show them the futility in sitting still and they'll see they have no choice but to try to rush me,* he thought. *That's my best chance at getting out of here alive.*

As he sat mulling over the status of his present situation, quietly sending occasional small puffs of smoke from behind his granite fortress, the shooting stopped, and he thought he heard two sets of boots running in his direction. He'd wait until the last minute to make his move. He knew he had to be deadly accurate if he was to mount a surprise attack that would end in his favor. As he heard the men pounding down the slope toward him, he prepared to gauge his response time to the precise second his attackers would be in the open and no more than ten or twelve feet away.

The moment arrived. Kelly spun out from behind the boulder, the Colt in his hand, and rose to face two men racing toward him, off balance, and caught in the open only a few feet away. It took only two quick shots to put an end to the ambush they had laid for him, slammed to earth by well-placed .44s. In an instant they both lay unmoving on the ground, trails of scarlet spreading across their sweat-soaked shirts. Kelly looked around for any others, but neither saw nor heard another sound. He was surrounded by an eerie silence. The whole desert seemed to see the deaths of the two cowboys as a signal to fall silent, to mourn the passing of human souls by adopting the doleful silence of a wake. Even the breeze had ceased as if in a moment of prayer.

Chapter Six

Kelly rounded up the horses of the two dead men. He hefted their bodies up and draped them across their saddles, tied them on securely with their own ropes, and began the slow trek back to the Pearson ranch house to return Silver's hirelings for a proper burial. He was greeted by three cowboys and Silver Pearson, himself, as he led the horses carrying their grisly burdens.

"What the hell is this? You kill these men?" he growled at Kelly, who had quickly dismounted and handed the other horses' reins to the nearest hand.

Kelly walked straight for Silver, causing the man to unconsciously take a step back and place his hand on the butt of his revolver.

"Yes, I shot these two ambushers, and I wouldn't go

for that hogleg if I were you. I'm in no mood to put up with any more attempts on my life today."

"What! You sayin' these boys took a shot at you?"

"That's what I'm sayin'. Now, why'd you send them out after me?"

Kelly reached over and slid his Winchester from its saddle scabbard. He chambered a round, keeping it pointed directly at Silver's stomach.

"I'm waiting for an answer," Kelly said. His look was dark, and deadly serious.

"They must have gone off on their own, thinkin' it was somethin' I'd approve of. But I didn't send 'em. They just got the wrong impression. Ain't neither of these young hotheads ever been too smart. I, uh, I'm sorry if they caused you any grief. Won't happen again," said Silver as he glanced at his other men. They grumbled at seeing their saddle-mates trussed up and dangling like freshly killed mule deer.

"No, sir, it surely won't. And if I find out you know more about the murder of that man up at Daleville that you aren't tellin' me, I'll be back. And you won't like that, either." With that, Kelly swung into the saddle, wheeled the gelding around and rode off at a trot. He glanced back to see the others gathered around their leader. He had a feeling he hadn't seen the last of that bunch.

Kelly's journey back to Purdy was uneventful. When he got to town, he rode straight to the constable's office. He tied his horse to the hitching rail and went inside.

He found the bulky lawman sitting at his desk, a knife in one hand, a fork in the other, and a mouthful of skillet steak.

"Got some extra, Marshal. Join me?"

"No, thanks. I just got back from the Pearson ranch. Didn't get a very warm reception. Two Pearson hirelings tried to bushwhack me. I had to kill them. Silver's not happy about that. You might want to keep your eye out for him to come lookin' to even the score on somebody."

The constable nodded with a scowl and a sigh. Kelly could see the constable was no match for Silver or anybody else with a yearning to shoot up the town. The best Jackson could do would be to keep out of sight until the shooting was over, and then clean up the mess. Kelly realized the moment he'd said it that his words were falling on deaf ears. He could only hope he hadn't loosed a rattler on the nearly defenseless town.

"Why do you figure he'd go and do a thing like that?"

"I don't know, but I think it may have to do with Albert Bourbonette, and the watch you found on Gold's body."

"Hmm. I wouldn't put robbery past them Pearson boys. It sounds like you figure Gold was involved, but is there some evidence that Silver or some of the others had anything to do with it?"

"I don't know what to think. If Silver hadn't sent two of his men to drygulch me, I'd have said he didn't know anything about it. But now, I have to wonder."

The constable sliced off another bite and stuffed it in his mouth, chewing with his mouth open. He took a swig of coffee, wiped his mouth with a red-checked napkin, and leaned back in his chair. It squeaked from the weight of his bulk.

"Is there anything else you can tell me about Silver?" said Kelly.

"Not much more than the obvious fact that they can't be makin' that poor piece of land out there pay. I can't prove it, but it seems to me that they 'bout have to be robbin' banks, or rustlin' cattle—certainly somethin' illegal. But I can't prove a bit of it. So, I just sit here and wait until somebody brings me something more than speculation. Even then, I ain't sure I can do a damn thing about it. I'd just be one old man against a hard-ened bunch of gunslingers."

Kelly got up and left with a thank you. He headed straight for Maggie's boarding house in hopes he wasn't too late for supper.

"Them damned fools. I should have sent somebody that could have got the job done instead of a couple of worthless fools. Bury 'em. I swear I'd give a hundred dollars to anyone who'd get the law out of my hair for a spell." Silver just shook his head and stormed off to the main house, letting the door slam behind him like a rifle shot.

One of Silver's men, a half-breed named Joseph Two Bears, leaned against a rickety bunk. He saw Silver's words as an opportunity. He brushed a shock of black hair out of his face as he slipped out of the bunkhouse alone and went for his horse. He checked his sidearm to be sure it was loaded, then swung into the saddle, and spurred the mare to a run towards Purdy. No one noticed he had left as the others gathered shovels to bury the men Kelly had bested.

When Two Bears got to Purdy, he went directly to the saloon. He stopped at the door for a moment, scanning the place with a slow, icy perusal. Seeing only one sleeping drunk, he entered and strolled to the bar.

"Beer," he said.

The bartender approached him slowly, wiping a tall glass with a damp bar towel.

"Two Bears, you know the last time I served you, all hell broke loose. You got stinkin' drunk, tore up the place, and damned near killed a man. You *do* remember spending several nights in jail, don't you? Maybe you ought to consider a sarsaparilla. What do you say?"

"Beer." Two Bears backed up his request by putting his hand on the Colt .44 that resided in a cross-draw holster.

The bartender looked resigned to an ugly situation, as he turned with a sigh and drew off a glass of beer from a keg at the end of the bar. He slid it down in front of Two Bears, trying to keep his distance as much as possible. Two Bears gulped the beer, then pounded the bar.

"Another beer."

This time, after drawing the foamy brew and sliding it down in front of the Indian, the bartender slipped out the back door and went to the constable's office.

"That fool Two Bears is back, and he's drinking. What'll I do?"

The constable rose slowly from his chair, pulled a shotgun from a rack behind him, and lumbered toward the door.

"Go over to Maggie's place and tell that marshal to meet me at the saloon. Tell him I could use a hand. Now hurry on over there," Constable Jackson said, as he squeezed through the narrow doorway, stomping along the boardwalk toward the Sure Shot Saloon.

Jackson pushed open the doors and shouted, "Two Bears, what the hell are you doin' back here? Don't you—"

His words had barely left his lips when Two Bears spun around, drew his revolver without a moment's hesitation, and shot Jackson. The big man went down hard, grasping his beefy thigh where the bullet had entered, leaving a growing red splotch on his wool pants. He rolled back and forth, groaning and bleeding on the wood floor. Two Bears turned back to finish his beer. Noticing that the bartender was missing, he went to the beer keg and drew another. He gulped it down and scooted out the back door just before Kelly and the bartender came busting in the front way.

Seeing the badly wounded Constable Jackson on the

floor, Kelly sent the bartender for someone to patch up the lawman. He looked about the room for someone who had seen where the shooter had gone. A man who had been asleep at a table near the back hollered from the dark corner that he had seen Two Bears run out the back, but that he hadn't been aware of any confrontation between the breed and the constable. Until the gunshot woke him up, he'd been oblivious to his surroundings.

"What happened, Jackson?" said Kelly.

"Damned if I know. That gun-crazy fool just up and plugged me," groaned the constable.

With his Winchester in hand, cocked and at the ready, Kelly slammed out the back door. The alley was empty. A noisy group had gathered out front after hearing the gunshot, but no one went inside for fear of getting involved in something that was none of their affair. As Kelly came around the side of the saloon, he stopped and asked if anyone had seen a man ride off recently. No one had.

Returning to the saloon, Kelly bent over the constable whose bleeding had slowed. A tourniquet had been applied by the barber, Carl Colville, the closest thing the town had to a doctor.

"We're going to need to get him over to my place so's I can remove that bullet, but I can't drag him there all by myself," said the barber. "Some of you heft him up and follow me. Be quick about it, now, before the man bleeds to death."

Seven men struggled in their attempt to lift the

groaning constable onto their shoulders, stumbling beneath the weight almost as if they had imbibed too much whiskey. But while it took so many men to get Jackson across the street and onto a table at the barber's shop, get him there they did without further damage.

The barber commenced to gathering his tools. He instructed one of the men to fetch him a bottle of whiskey to get the constable lathered up a bit to help ease the pain. Jackson took several gulps from the pale red whiskey, as he showed nervousness at the prospects of being carved on by a barber playing doctor.

After the operation, Colville proudly announced that he had successfully removed the bullet, stitched up the hole, and bandaged the leg, and would happily accept any and all drinks that might be bestowed upon him by a grateful town. A boisterous crowd accompanied the barber to the saloon for the occasion, as the bleary-eyed constable lay humming to himself on the barber's table, oblivious to much of anything after consuming two shots of whiskey and a thimbleful of laudanum, given him to ease the pain.

Kelly figured the shooter might still be in town, so he began a door-by-door search. When he reached the livery, however, his quest came to an abrupt end, for, as he eased inside the great double doors, he was greeted by a sudden blow to the back of his head. He went down, unable to catch more than a glimpse of his attacker before he blacked out.

Two Bears had saddled a horse and was getting set to leave town without further delay. His own horse was still tied up outside the saloon, but he would have been a fool to walk back through a crowd of angry citizens to retrieve it. He mounted up, and rode out the back way, adding assault and horse theft to what would surely be charges of attempted murder of a lawman. Joseph Two Bears was well on his way to becoming a legend in this part of the territory, and, to his mind, one hundred dollars richer.

That is, of course, if he managed to live long enough to spend it.

Chapter Seven

Jed and Jake Bourbonette had just finished off their complimentary bottle of sherry in their Tucson hotel room when there came a knock at their door. Jake opened it to find himself facing a burly sheriff's deputy.

"Good afternoon, Deputy. What can I do for you?" Jake said.

"I come to take you over for a sit-down with Sheriff Smith. He would've come hisself but he's been feelin' a mite poorly of late," said the deputy.

"Why would he be interested in talking to me?"

"I figure it's about that card game you was involved in with a local fella earlier today. That fella has some kinda beef with you, and since he's the sheriff's cousin, I reckon you best get yourself on over to his office."

"I'm afraid you have the wrong man, Deputy. I'm

not very good at cards. You want to talk to my brother, Jed." And with that, he opened the door wide enough for the deputy to see Jed practicing some fancy card rolls at the table.

The deputy looked first to one, then the other. He stepped inside, removed his hat, and addressed a nonchalant Jed who barely acknowledged the deputy's presence.

"Sir, I'm Deputy Simpson, and the sheriff has sent me to fetch you on over to his office for a talk."

"I already heard you telling my brother. You can go back and inform the sheriff that I'll be by a bit later in the day, after the heat has slacked off some," said Jed, cutting the deck with one hand.

"I'll be sure to tell him, but I don't think he had in mind waitin' around. He's not a man to trifle with when it comes to holdin' a gun on his kinfolk and robbin' them. If I was you, I'd git on over there and straighten this out before he gets too hot under the collar."

With that, Deputy Simpson left the room. Jake closed the door behind him. He then turned to his brother.

"You said you out-played that fool gambler. You didn't say nothin' about robbin' him. What do we do now?"

"Calm yourself, brother. I'll handle it. But it'll be on my terms, not the sheriff's."

"Jed, you're forgetting what we came here to do. We're supposed to be finding the men who killed our brother, that's all. I want to get back to my store, and do it with a minimum of trouble. I can't run a business from a jail cell. Now get on over there and talk to that sheriff."

Jed didn't even look up to acknowledge his brother's admonition to get the problem solved, and to do it before it spilled over into real trouble. He just sat there, flipping cards, trying to call them before he turned them over. He shuffled, cut, then did it all over again. To Jed's mind, he had been in the right calling out the gambler's cheating. The man had it coming to him, whatever he got. From Jake's point of view, his brother had become a scofflaw, and he wasn't having any of it.

Bothered by his brother's disdain of the law, Jake moved to take matters into his own hands. He took his hat from the table, and left the hotel room in a huff. When he got to the bottom of the stairs, he asked of the desk clerk where he might find the sheriff's office. Before leaving, he turned back to the clerk.

"Sir, would you happen to know the relationship between the sheriff and a local gambler, a man who has his hair slicked-down and wears a red cravat?"

"Oh, you mean Driscol. Yeah, I know him. All the locals know to stay away from that thieving scoundrel. He's kin of the sheriff's. Although, I don't know how much love there is between them. Driscol's been accused of just about everything a man can be and still not get hanged for it."

"If Driscol is such a sidewinder, why does the sheriff cover for him? Why isn't the man in jail?"

"Blood's thicker'n water, or so they say. And Driscol is the sheriff's wife's first cousin. I reckon he don't want to tip over the slop barrel where he eats."

Jake thought about that for a moment, then went outside. He walked toward the sheriff's office, following the directions given him by the hotel clerk. When he reached the door, he hesitated a moment before entering, not completely certain what he was going to say in his brother's defense. But if Jed wasn't going to come as the sheriff requested, someone had to save him from his folly. He turned the handle and stepped inside.

"Sheriff Smith, my name is Jake Bourbonette. I believe you asked my brother to come over for a chat. He is tied up at the moment, so I thought I'd stop in just so's you'd know you weren't being snubbed," said Jake, his hat in his hand.

The sheriff was a ruddy-complexioned man with dark circles under his eyes, a long, gaunt face, and gray hair that had receded significantly. He looked up over a pair of Franklin glasses, then returned to writing on a piece of paper. The scratching of the pen set Jake's nerves on edge, as if he needed any help. Finally, after letting Jake cool his heels for several minutes, the sheriff removed his glasses and looked Jake squarely in the eye.

"Well, here's the way I see it. I'm told your brother held a gun on my wife's cousin, a worthless, no-good, crooked sidewinder with a compulsion to gamble and steal other people's hard-earned money. Can't keep his hands off the pasteboards. I'm darned sure he had it comin' because he's cheated his way across the territory and back. He ought to be in jail. But, as I said, he *is* my wife's cousin, so I'm in a pickle. You got any suggestions, son?"

Jake was surprised by the sheriff's outspokenness. He frowned as he searched for the right words in answer to the man's question. He saw this as an opportunity to salvage at least a portion of what Jed took from the gambler, and maybe not lose it all. That's when the solution came to him. But it was imperative to choose carefully the next words that came out of his mouth.

"Well, sir, as a point of fact, my brother is a very accomplished gambler, and he doesn't have to stick a gun in a man's face to come out a winner. Jed, that's my brother, and I watched as this Driscol fella cleaned out a couple of poor cowboys who didn't have a lick of sense when it come to tossin' around their pay. So when they walked away broke, Jed said he'd like to have a go at the gambler. That's when I left. When Jed returned to our hotel room, he said he didn't even have to cheat since he caught this Driscol with a card up his sleeve. Now if that isn't robbery, I don't know what is. I'd say he was just gettin' back what was stole from him. If he got a little more than his due, well, I suspect he'd see himself clear to turn over a bit of it to you for your kind understanding," said Jake.

The sheriff leaned back, cocked his head to one side and raised his eyebrows.

"Well, young man, perhaps you have just come up with the perfect solution to a complex issue. I figure I could see my way to twenty-five percent of the takings, if your brother could see *his* way to that, and if he'd agree to no more gamblin' with Driscol, I'd call the matter settled."

"That sounds like a fair proposition, Sheriff. I'm certain I can get my brother to fork over the money. I'll just take my leave and return soon with the proceeds, if that suits you."

The sheriff grinned as he waved Jake off, obviously well pleased by the plan with which he'd been presented.

Jake hurried down the street, heading straight for the hotel. He took the stairs two at a time. He was almost out of breath when he turned the knob to the room. Jed was still turning cards as Jake entered, panting. He didn't look up.

"Okay, Jed, I've come up with a deal to get the law off your back for robbing that gambler Driscol. Where's the cash you took off him?"

"In my coat pocket, right where it's going to stay."

"Not all of it, I'm afraid."

"Now just what do you mean by that?"

"I've just promised the sheriff twenty-five percent of

it to keep him off your back for holdin' a gun on that thief Driscol."

"Now hold on, brother . . ."

Jake's usually calm demeanor disappeared suddenly, as if blown away by a strong wind, and his face grew red. He slammed his fist down on the table that separated them.

"Listen, I've just saved your bacon, and there'll be no buts about it. I'm closin' the deal I made with the sheriff and that's that. I won't listen to another word out of you on the issue. We came here to get the snakes that shot our brother, and by damned, that's what we're goin' to do," growled Jake.

Jed was making no headway defying his brother. Clearly, twenty-five percent as a sort of commission paid to the sheriff wasn't all that bad a deal. Especially if none of it would ever grace the pockets of that crooked gambler.

"Okay. I can see your reasoning. Go ahead and take the share you promised the law. I'll meet you out front, we'll get ourselves a bite to eat, and then we'll start our search for them varmints that shot poor Albert," said Jed.

With that, Jed returned to his shuffling and rolling the deck of cards in front of him. He had a darkly satisfied look on his face as Jake fumbled through the coat pocket and came out with a wad of bills. Jed watched out of the corner of his eye as Jake straightened each bill, counted it, and then divvied it up into two piles, taking the short stack and stuffing it into his own pocket. Jake left without another word.

When Kelly came to, he rolled over slowly in a painful attempt to get to his feet. He felt the back of his head and came away with a bloody hand. He stumbled to the door, leaned on it for support for a moment, then proceeded to the barber's storefront. On the way, a man rushed up to him.

"Marshal, you hurt?"

"A little crack on the head. Did anyone see where that half-breed went?"

"Saw him hightailin' it out of town a few minutes ago."

"Did it look like he was goin' back to the Pearson place?"

"More like southeast, out across the chaparral. 'Spect he's goin' to see if he can make it to Black Skull Canyon. That's sure where I'd head for if I just shot a constable and busted open a marshal's head. The boy ain't bright, you know."

"Why do you suppose he shot Jackson? Did he have a beef with him?"

"Two Bears is just a hot-head. Gets a little liquor in him, and he seems to turn into a banshee. But then, like I said, he ain't bright. I reckon he ain't forgot last month when the constable put him up in the steel-door hotel for gettin' drunk and passin' out in the middle of the street."

When they reached the barber's door, the man walked away with a wave. Kelly went inside to find a groaning constable continuing his repose on the table, several bloody cloths on the floor, and the barber trying to lift the constable's sizable thigh high enough to wrap a clean cloth around it.

"How's it look for Jackson, Mister Colville?"

Colville looked up from his struggle with the bandaging just enough to notice the blood on the marshal's hand.

"Looks like you met up with the Indian, too. Better let me take a look."

Kelly sat down in the barber chair and closed his eyes as Colville wrung out a wet cloth and tried to clean the wound. He clucked his tongue at the sight.

"Got you a good one, Marshal. Nasty cut, but I think you'll be all right after a little rest. I'll fix you right up."

"If he'd hit me with a rifle butt, I'd probably be dead. You take care of Jackson. I'll be fine, just need to sit a spell."

The barber poured some alcohol on a cloth and pressed it to Kelly's wound. The sting of the alcohol opened his eyes in a hurry.

"Here, hold this to your head for a few minutes. I'll see if I need to do a little sewin' as soon as I finish with the constable."

Kelly decided after a few minutes of soaking the wound in alcohol, he wasn't quite ready to let the barber take a needle and thread to him. He got up, took his rifle, and bade Colville goodbye. The barber tried to protest such a hasty decision, but Kelly was already outside and headed for Maggie's boarding house before Colville could get out more than a dozen mumbled words.

Chapter Eight

Kelly winced as Maggie worked on his lacerated head.

"He cracked you a good one, Marshal. But don't you worry none, I'll have you good as new in no time." She applied some dark brown salve to the broken skin and wrapped a clean cloth around his head.

"Might be hard to get your hat on for a few days, but you'll mend," she said with a motherly smile and a chuckle.

"Thank you, ma'am. I had a feeling I'd be better off takin' my chances with you." He picked up his cavalry-style Stetson, struggled to get his sea legs, and went to his room. He sat on the edge of the bed for a few minutes, his chin in his hands, elbows on his knees. He needed a few minutes to clear his head of the fog that seemed to envelope him like low clouds in the mountains. His head was still spinning when he lay back, and promptly drifted off to sleep.

The aroma of coffee wafting through the hallway woke him up much later. He got to his feet, splashed water on his face from the basin, and made his way to the dining room. There was only one other man sitting at the table. Seth Bonner looked up as Kelly entered the room pale and bleary-eyed.

"Heard about Jackson getting himself shot by that crazy Indian. Looks like he got a chunk of you, too."

"Hmm."

"Well, if you've a mind to go after him, you'd best watch your back 'cause he's got kin in them hills. That's where he heads for every time there's trouble," said Bonner.

With some effort, Kelly smiled as Maggie poured him a cup of steaming coffee, and placed a plate of fresh bread and home-churned butter in front of him.

"The real food's almost ready, gents," she said, and promptly turned on her heel and left the room.

"What do you know about this man? I think Jackson said his name is Joseph Two Bears."

"Yep, that's it all right. But we just call him Two Bears. Been out at the Pearson place for 'bout a year and a half. Gold, Silver, Galt, Two Bears, and Daniel Free take off every now and then for who knows where or why. All I know is, they don't raise enough cattle out at that place to feed themselves for more'n a month. So they's up to no good, I can almost guarantee it, and there ain't a good one in the bunch. But they keep comin' into town to spend money, so folks put up with their strange ways," Bonner said. "Near everyone in town feels the same about them."

"What do you know about Two Bears' kin? Where can I find them?"

"Well, the white side of his family got themselves a small ranch just this side of the cliffs. Mostly rustlers. When it looks like the law is closing in, they all skedaddle over into Black Skull Canyon, that maze of switchbacks, sheer rock faces, abandoned mines, and sinkholes every other ornery cuss ridin' the owlhoot trail holes up in when they's on the run. Ought to be called Drygulch Canyon."

Kelly ate slowly, letting the fine flavor of Maggie's beef stew help soothe the dull ache in his head, hoping to let the one overcome the other. He slipped deep into thought about what Seth Bonner had told him about Two Bears, a warning that carried more than just the casual admonition to take care. The man's expression in the way he told it made him more cautious than he otherwise might be. Kelly had always been one to be more decisive than pensive, more active than passive, more passionate than blasé. The tone of Bonner's disquieting forewarning carried with it the not-so-subtle suggestion to consider a preparedness that might otherwise have been overlooked.

"Tell me whatever you know about Two Bears.

Where'd he come from? Has he ever been wanted for anything? Where is the Indian side of his family?" Kelly asked.

"Whoa, Marshal. I know a fair amount of what passes for fact hereabouts, but I'm no en-cy-clo-pedia. Far as where he come from, I don't rightly know." Bonner scratched his head, frowned, then scrunched up his face. "There's some talk he is half Kiowa, but others say Comanche. One fella came in one day griping about that damned Arapaho, Two Bears. Your guess is as good as mine as to which side of the covers his papa come from."

"Got any idea why he drew down on Jackson?"

"All I know is, that Indian can get drunker'n a Saturday night cowboy by just sniffin' alcohol. Got no tolerance, whatsoever. I 'spect he just was overcome by the beer, 'cause I don't know of any special dislike he has for Jackson, except of course for the times the Indian has spent the night in jail for gettin' on the wrong side of a bottle."

"Why didn't the bartender just refuse to serve him off?"

"'Cause he can be meaner than a skunk, and he don't seem to have no qualms about pullin' that hogleg on a man, neither."

"Thanks. I appreciate your help," said Kelly. He returned to scratching around in his plate. The food was good, but the pain in his head had dampened his appetite. That, and his eagerness to get on Two Bear's trail had taken away some of his interest in eating.

After a few minutes, Kelly took his rifle, which was leaning against the wall behind his chair, and went back to his room, well aware he was in no shape to commence a ride this late in the day, and with a lump on his head the size of an egg. *Tomorrow will be plenty of time to start the chase,* he talked himself into believing.

About a mile from town, Two Bears swung around to head directly for the Pearson ranch to collect his due and gather up his belongings before moving east towards Black Skull Canyon. When he got there, Silver was standing at the door to the ranch house, smoking a cigarillo. He called out to Two Bears from the shadows.

"Hey. Over here, Injun. Where you been?" Silver called out.

"Went to town like you said. I did what you said to do. I'll be ridin' for the canyon soon's I get my beddin'." Two Bears dismounted, and started for the bunkhouse.

"What did I say to do? Say, you didn't do nothin' to bring the law back out here, did you?"

"I shot the constable. I also brought that marshal down with the butt of my gun. Don't figure either one will be too eager to come snoopin' around here anytime soon. But I figure to head on out, draw any posse that might come lookin' away from here. You won't be involved, Mister Pearson. So, if you'll just give me the one hundred dollars you promised to slow down the law in Purdy, I'll be on my way."

"You damned fool. They know where you work. Git

on outta here. And don't come back, you hear! I've had all I can stomach of your wild Injun ways."

"I'll just get my gear and go. And how about my money?"

Silver drew his sidearm.

"You'll take nothin', and there'll be no money. Now, git before I put a bullet where your brain outta be. If you *ever* had a brain."

"But, Mister Silver, I need my blankets. I could freeze out there at night."

Silver cocked his revolver and aimed it at Two Bears.

"I never meant for nobody to get shot you fool. You brought this on yourself. Now, I said move!" said Silver.

Reluctantly, Two Bears got back on his horse and spurred his mount to a run toward the gate and his hope of escape from the law. His anger at being treated the way he had by Silver caught in his throat. After all the times he'd ridden side-by-side with Silver and his brother, Gold, to be shown the door for what he saw as a legitimate offer of reward to get rid of the law brought thoughts of revenge quickly to mind.

After leaving the ranch property, he slowed his horse to a trot. He needed time to think. He had to find a way to get back at the man he'd shared so many crimes with, and who had now thrown him to the wolves. And that same man had his full share of the plunder that the Pearson gang had amassed over the past year-and-a-half still sitting in a tin box back at the ranch. All along, he'd been given scraps to keep him satisfied, just enough to buy necessities and an occasional drink, but always with the promise of the whole amount due him to be paid out as soon as things cooled down and they were sure the law wasn't on their trail.

Now, things looked bad for Two Bears ever seeing his share, what with Gold getting gunned down over a faro game. And no one knew who the two men were that did the killing, nor why they seemed to be after Gold in the first place. And now Silver had tossed him off the ranch.

He rode up into the foothills to consider his plight. He found a place where he had a good view of the road and anyone either coming to or from the ranch. He staked his horse out near a creek. He then hunkered down behind some boulders, pulled his knees up and set to thinking hard on all that had happened. He wasn't stupid, or touched in the head as so many had suggested; he just had a terrible weakness for whiskey or beer. His drinking had been a problem, and he didn't know how to fend off those demons when they called him. Whenever he heard those whispers that drew him back to a saloon, he knew it was like walking blindfolded into a rattler's den.

As he wrestled with his dilemma, his anger grew. He didn't have to take this kind of treatment from anyone. And he sure wasn't going to allow Silver to take what rightfully belonged to him. He risked his own life to steal from others, now he was being stolen from. He had always done what Silver had wanted, followed orders completely, and now he was being rejected for it. He could simply not abide such treatment, which, he reasoned, came about solely because he was half Indian. The longer he dwelled on it, the deeper his anger grew. There was no two ways about it, he had to respond in kind to Silver's attempt to cut him out of his due.

And so, he drew himself up straight and threw out his chest, allowing pride to rule his feelings, and give him the strength to do what he knew must be done. He'd tried on many occasions to reason things out when a problem presented itself. But this time, he would not try to grapple with common sense. He would follow his instincts, and strike the first blow. His first thought was to sneak back into the ranch compound and maybe enlist Daniel Free to help him retrieve some of the bounty from Silver's safe. Perhaps even become a full-fledged partner and steal it all for themselves. Maybe they could light out for New Mexico, perhaps all the way up to Santa Fe, where the senoritas were beautiful, dark-skinned, and they didn't look upon his mixed ancestry with disdain, as the women did in Purdy.

Two Bears' dark eyes flashed with determination as he gathered in the reins of the horse he'd stolen in his haste to get out of Purdy. He was a small man, and he was more comfortable on the paint pony that had been given him by his Kiowa relatives than on the larger horses the cowboys rode. He was angry that he'd had to leave his pony. As he started to mount up, he thought he saw a trail of dust far off to the west, coming from the direction of town. He stopped, led his mount back behind the rocks to wait and watch, just to make certain it wasn't the marshal coming to gun him down for shooting the constable. He waited as the dust cloud disappeared as quickly as it had appeared. No rider, just the wind whipping up a dust devil. His nerves were getting the best of him. He'd started imagining things.

Climbing back on his mount, he grumbled to himself at how stupid he'd been to believe Silver would be straight with him. Now, he could be looking at prison time, or worse, a rope. Perspiration began to run off his forehead.

Chapter Nine

Marshal Kelly gathered his belongings and stuffed them into his saddlebags in preparation to track Two Bears. He wasn't happy that he'd been drawn into having to chase down a fugitive for what was plainly a local crime, diverted from the real purpose of his having come to Purdy in the first place. The time it would take to track and apprehend the half-breed gunman was time he didn't have if ever he was to figure out the whole story behind the murder of Albert Bourbonette. But, maybe Two Bears' brush with the law wasn't so local after all, he thought, as he fingered the bump on the back of his head, glad it had been only a glancing blow. He could be dead.

The morning sky had dawned bright and cloudless. It was certain to be an unbearably hot ride out to the

Pearson ranch, and Kelly's throbbing head wouldn't make the trip any easier. It wouldn't have taken much for him to give up the chase and just take it easy for a few more days, giving his cracked skull more time to heal. Maggie's home cooking seemed to have a recuperative effect. But he owed it to Constable Jackson to bring in the man who had shot him, possibly leaving the constable a cripple for the rest of his life.

So, when he found Maggie sitting on the front porch peeling potatoes, he tipped his hat and told her he'd be back in a couple of days, if all went the way he planned. She gave him a questioning glance, as if he'd lost his mind going off without sufficient time to heal. But Maggie was not one to meddle in the business of others. She just gave him a sympathetic smile and wished him god-speed.

Kelly was well aware that the main trail to the Pearson ranch would take him past the place where he was ambushed before. He was also aware of the possibility that regardless of which direction he appeared to have headed, Two Bears would circle around and head for the ranch, either to get help from the other hands in thwarting Kelly's attempt to bring him in, or to stock up on supplies before heading into the fiery furnace that lay to the east, the devil's own mountainous hideaway for thieves and rustlers. He had warned Silver against any further attempts by his men to disrupt his investigation. But would the man heed his warning?

Armed with two canteens, Kelly struck out on a

southerly, more roundabout route that would lead him down a dry creek bed that wandered through the low hills, which, during the monsoon season, flowed freely with welcome water from the mountains to the east. While taking the direct route to the Pearson ranch would be easier going and considerably quicker, Kelly was not feeling up to another tangle with some owlhoot sitting up in the rocks waiting to pick him off with a rifle. The meandering way he chose had few, if any, places to conceal a man bent on ambush as it led through land that climbed slowly to the foothills, populated with little more than low scrub.

The desert was full of life and color as he rode among bright blooming barrel cacti and watched butterflies flittering about seeking the sweet nectar of the snakeweed. He even caught sight of an occasional Gila monster lumbering across the sands. Kelly welcomed the August monsoons as they brought the desert alive with vivid colors, and the sounds of birds singing their approval of the occasional respite from blistering heat. In fact, he found the presence of desert sounds to be a good indicator that nothing was amiss. An eerie silence hangs over the land whenever men with guns lie in wait for an unsuspecting passerby. But today, he heard sounds and songs aplenty, and was heartened that he had chosen a route to the Pearson ranch that should circumvent any such treachery.

Jed and Jake Bourbonette pushed through the doors to the fanciest saloon in town, aware they were under the scrutiny of every person, either leaning back in a chair at a table strewn with cards, or hanging on the bar, one boot hiked up on the brass rail. By reclaiming the money he'd lost to the notoriously crooked gambler, Driscol, Jed had gained an unexpected respect from the local citizenry, many of whom had fallen victim to the unscrupulous gambler in the past. And since Driscol was related to Sheriff Smith, no one expected to ever see *their* money again. But word had it that the sheriff had warned his cousin against any further gambling in Tucson. He reportedly told him to take his crooked game down to Bisbee, or Douglas, or one of the many smaller towns that were strewn about the southeastern part of the territory like tumbleweeds, popping up at the first hint of gold, copper, or silver, then disappearing as soon as the last ounce of color could be plucked from the ground.

"Look at the way these men are staring at us, Jake. Makes a man feel proud, don't it? They're thinking I'm some sort of hero, or something."

"Yeah, well if it hadn't been for me, you'd be a hero sitting in jail right now, and no tellin' how long you'd be there. Probably until you rotted," said Jake.

"I said 'Thank you' didn't I? You don't have to keep rubbing it in."

"Let's get a beer and work out a plan for finding the other three men that killed Albert," said Jake.

They scooted two chairs out at a table near the front of the long hall. The bartender came over and asked what they'd like, and soon came back with two beers overflowing with frothy foam. He returned to his position of authority behind the bar as Jake leaned over to his brother and began to whisper.

"First, I want to know what makes you think they may have come here. We're pretty far from our ranch, and Tucson seems an unlikely hiding place. That fella living in Purdy made more sense," said Jake.

"All right, I'll tell you. Before I came back to Daleville, I'd been working the riverboats up and down the Mississippi. I was doin' pretty well, too. But one day I overheard a fella from Tucson talkin' about some men he knew who liked to hit ranches east along the San Pedro, robbing them mostly during the daytime while folks were working fence lines or tending cattle. Made a fair haul, too, accordin' to the one doin' all the talkin'. It never meant much to me until you told me about Albert and the ranch when I returned. So, I figured this would be a good place to start lookin' for those owlhoots."

As the brothers were locked in conversation, a man entered the saloon and strode to the bar. He wore a floppy-brimmed hat with a single silver concho on the hatband. In the middle of the concho was a polished piece of turquoise. The man's deeply lined face was almost obscured by a graying mustache and thin beard, and long, stringy hair that flowed to his shoulders. Deep-set eyes looked at no one. He ordered a whisky, downed it in one gulp, ordered another, and did the same. Then, without a word, dropped two coins on the bar and strode out.

Jed had watched the man every second he was inside. Then, after the man exited through the swinging doors, he whispered to his brother, "Don't that man kinda resemble the description you gave me of one of Albert's killers, although without the beard and mustache? What do you think?"

"Yeah. I reckon he sorta looks like he could be one of them. The descriptions the sheriff got were a little vague, but that long hair sounds right. I'd be in favor of following him for a spell. Maybe we can get a better look at him outside in the sunlight. He might even do or say something to give himself away," said Jake.

They stood up and pushed through the doors to follow the long-haired man. They spotted him nearly a half-block away, where he'd have been lost amongst the many people coming in and out of shops were it not for his being almost half a head taller than most.

"There he is, down by the gunsmith's. Jake, you go across the street and try to stay with him, but don't make it obvious you're following him. That way you'll have the best view of any store he goes into, and also he won't be apt to notice he's being followed. Two men walking together, and coming his way, might tip him off. I'll stay on this side, and keep some of the townsfolk between us."

Jake crossed the busy street and clomped up onto the boardwalk. He stopped occasionally, glancing in windows or making it appear he was striking up a quick, casual conversation with one of the many men sitting under porch overhangs or canvas awnings outside the barber shop or the hotel. He could clearly see the stranger entering the gunsmith's shop.

Jake waved to his brother, then sat on a bench to await the man's next move. Nearly twenty minutes passed before the man came out of the gunsmith's. He sauntered across the street to the same hotel where the Bourbonettes were staying. Jed joined his brother on the bench.

"Well, do we brace him, or watch what he does for awhile?"

"I got a funny feelin' about that hombre. I say we go talk to that gunsmith. See what he knows," said Jake.

Jed grunted a vague approval, and the two of them headed for the gunsmith's shop.

"Howdy, gents. What can I do for you?"

"We saw a man come out of here a few minutes ago. Thought he looked some like a long lost cousin. Long hair, gray mustache, and beard. You happen to know his name?" said Jake.

"Hardly anyone around these parts don't know Preacher Ben Cutter," said the gunsmith.

"He a rancher?"

"A rancher? Ha! That's a good one. If I were you, I'd stay as far away from that rattler as I could get. He'd just as soon blow you to kingdom come as look at you."

"You mean he's a gunfighter?" said Jed.

"He's a mite more than a gunfighter. He's a killer, plain and simple. Makes the likes of Clay Allison look tame. Don't want to get him riled, boys, unless you have a hankerin' to bleed all over the street. Why, I heard tell Cutter backed down John Ringo with no more'n a snarl."

"Well, it's obvious this Mr. Cutter ain't the fella we thought he might be. Thanks for the advice, mister." Jed and Jake hurried from the gunsmith's shop, slipping into a saloon next door. After ordering a couple of whiskeys, Jake leaned over to his brother.

"It pays to know who you're goin' up against, brother. Why we could be lying dead out there in the dirt if we'd tried to go up against that man. Caution, that's what I been sayin' all along. We gotta be damn careful we got the right men before we go gettin' into something we can't finish."

Jed stared at the wall, his eyes glazed over as if he was in a trance. He didn't say a word for several minutes. Then, when he did speak, it was Jake's turn to go all pasty white.

"What if we enlisted that Cutter fellow in helpin' us search for the other three killers? How much do you s'pose he'd charge?" said Jed.

Jake just shook his head. "Jed, there are times when I think you're just plain crazy. Why, with thinkin' like that, you're gonna get us shot-up sure as hell. I'll have nothin' more to do with this whole deal if you so much as speak to that man. Do you understand?"

Jed shrugged his shoulders, but said nothing. He was too busy conjuring up a scheme to reply.

Chapter Ten

Two Bears huddled beneath a concave boulder, staying well back on the dirt floor beneath the cave-like overhang, nursing a growing anger at how he'd been cheated by Silver Pearson. He repeatedly cocked and released the hammer on his revolver, easing it down with his thumb as he pulled the trigger so as not to allow it to fire. Over and over he cocked and released, cocked and released, until he could no longer contain his rage. Suddenly he was driven to fire the revolver, fanning it again and again, into the ground, into the air, anywhere and nowhere, until he'd emptied the chamber. He dropped to his knees and pounded his fists on the ground with a scream of anguish. He then fell back against the rock face, spent of energy, but already conjuring a plan that would even the score with his former boss.

Kelly rode down into a draw where a thin ribbon of greenish water was all that remained of a stream winding through the rocks. A few small cottonwoods and some patchy grass struggled to maintain their tentative grip along the rocky banks. He dismounted to let the gelding get a drink as he picked out the closest tree for some shade. He drank from his canteen, then looked around for any signs of his not being alone. The only tracks he saw were those of thirsty javalina, coyote, and the occasional mule deer that came to sip from scattered pools of stagnant water. Up high in the cliffs above where he stood pondering his next move, he could see a natural path leading to the top. It looked like an excellent place to get a view of the valley and possibly the Pearson ranch below without his being seen.

Leaving his gelding to chomp on the clumps of grass and sip from the warm water, Kelly began the climb to the top. Careful to avoid any misstep that might send him on a painful journey to the bottom, he slowly made his way across loose gravel and patches of bare slickrock, sending pebbles skittering down the incline with each step. At the summit, he found he had a commanding view of not only the ranch house and outbuildings, but also the cluster of boulders and hills where the two

Pearson men had ambushed him. It was easy to see the short route they had taken to get there before he passed. He raised a pair of field glasses to his eye, adjusting them to focus on the farthest objects. It was from this vantage point that he saw tiny puffs of smoke rising from a cluster of far-off boulders. He could see no particular target for a shooter, so he just kept the glass trained on the rocks for several minutes in hopes of discovering who had been blowing off ammunition, and at what.

He didn't have to wait long, as a horse and rider emerged from amongst a cluster of boulders and headed toward the ranch at a dead run. As the rider got closer, Kelly had to figure it was probably Two Bears, although he had never gotten a good look at him before being driven to the floor by the half-breed's gun butt. He unconsciously rubbed the spot where Two Bears had struck him. The lump was still there, no bigger, no smaller. And still damned sore.

I think I'll just sit here and see what happens, he thought. *From the way he's riding, I'd say he might not be expecting a friendly reception.*

It didn't take long for Kelly's prediction to come true.

As soon as Two Bears got close enough to identify, three men piled out of the bunkhouse and ran to Silver Pearson's side in front of the ranch house. Each was armed as if he expected trouble. If he saw the gathering of ranch hands, Two Bears appeared to have paid no attention.

He just kept coming.

Two Bears made no attempt to even slow down at the sight of what awaited him. He pulled his rifle from its scabbard, stuffed the reins in his teeth, and lifted the Winchester to eye level. His first shot shattered a window right behind the group of men. That sent them scattering for cover, although there was little in the way of places nearby to hide from a fusillade of bullets fired by an angry and desperate man. Several of them scuttled around to the back of the house, another dropped to the ground, and another high-tailed it for the bunkhouse to retrieve something more suitable than a six-shooter. Silver Pearson stepped back inside the doorway.

Two Bears kept coming.

Pearson came back out into the light, armed this time with a Sharp's buffalo gun. He raised it to his cheek, sighted down through the stock-mounted sight, and pulled the trigger. A blast of grayish-white smoke engulfed him for a moment as the rifle bucked against his shoulder like the kick of a mule. But when the smoke had cleared sufficiently for him to see what he'd hit, he began fumbling to chamber another .50 caliber round. He hadn't hit anything but air.

The half-breed kept coming.

Two Bears cocked and fired the Winchester rapidly as he charged the house. Bullets careened off the stone building, shattering windows, keeping any man brave enough to stick his head around a corner convinced of the stupidity of such a move. Silver aimed again, and, in his haste to get off another shot before Two Bears was upon him, yanked the trigger too hard, pulling the shot harmlessly well off to the right of the oncoming rider. Silver was out of options, and he spun around to seek shelter inside once again. But he was too late. Two Bears' next bullet found its mark, slamming a screaming Silver Pearson to the ground from a .45 caliber hunk of lead that shattered his left leg. Leaning on one arm, he held up his other hand.

"Don't shoot no more. I'm finished. You don't need to kill me. I'll give you what you want." His strength spent, he dropped back into the dirt, groaning from the pain, his heaving breath blowing puffs of dust away from his mouth.

Two Bears reined in just short of his old boss, dismounted in a swirl of dust, and dropped to one knee, his rifle held at the ready.

"Call off your men, Silver, or I'll finish the job, here and now."

"All right. Just don't shoot," Silver pleaded.

"Do it!"

"Lay down your guns, boys. It's over," groaned Silver. "Don't try anything, just stay where you are."

"Where's my share of the loot, Silver, and my extra hundred dollars?" Two Bears reached down, grabbed Silver by the collar, and pulled him to a nearly sitting position.

"Inside, in a tin box in my desk. Help me up and I'll get it for you."

"Nothing doing. I don't trust you. I'll just get it myself. And it better be where you say it is." Two Bears let Silver drop back in the dirt, got up, and sprinted inside. His eyes fell to the carved oak desk in the middle of the main room. He yanked open a drawer and found nothing but a pile of papers. The second drawer yielded only a ledger of some sort. On his third try, however, he hit pay dirt. There in a tin box he found thousands of dollars in bills and coins. And, under the money lay a loaded double derringer. Two Bears' decision not to let Silver accompany him inside had proven a wise one.

Instead of counting out his share, he scooped up the whole box, as well as the ledger, and headed for the door, but not before chambering another round in the Winchester. Once burned, twice cautious, had been his mother's favorite dictum. It wasn't lost on Two Bears.

And, just as he suspected, Silver was waiting for him to emerge from the house. Two Bears ducked back instantly at the sight of the Sharps aimed in his direction. The blast blew a hole through the door big enough to put a fist through. Two Bears dove through the door and onto the porch. He pulled the trigger on the Winchester as he hit the planks. Silver Pearson didn't make a sound as the bullet thudded into his chest. He slumped back to the ground, killed by a single shot.

Two Bears sprinted for his horse, looking back as he

went to make sure none of the ranch hands were taking a bead on him. He mounted, fired one last shot in the direction of the bunkhouse as a warning not to follow, and spurred the bay to a run, away from the ranch, away from the man who had tried to cheat him, and who now lay dead in a pool of his own blood, all his ill-gotten gains forfeit to one of his own kind.

Kelly was startled at the scene that lay before him. From his vantage point it looked like Two Bears had killed his old boss, and lit out with something in his hand. He'd ridden away like his britches were afire, heading north at first, then turning east toward Black Skull Canyon. The marshal watched with interest at what might happen next when the ranch hands found their employer dead, the hand that fed them no longer up to the task. As Two Bears disappeared into the hills, and the shooting was over, several of Pearson's men did come running to where Silver lay. Kelly couldn't hear what they were saying, but from their hand gestures, there was some disagreement as to what course to take. This was as good a time as any to ride down and see what information he could pry out of any of them about the Bourbonette robbery and killing.

He slid down the incline, called to his foraging black gelding, and mounted up for the short ride to the ranch house. When he rode up, several of the men expressed surprise at seeing him, one or two others lit a shuck for their horses, mounted up, and left in a hurry by way of the front gate. Kelly dismounted, and strode up to the few who remained, gazing at their fallen employer. Most were in disbelief that something like this could have happened.

"Marshal, did you see Two Bears? He just gunned down Mister Pearson in cold blood. Never gave him a chance."

"Yeah, Marshal, I seen it all. Pearson had no chance at all. Murdered right here on his own spread."

"I *did* see it all from up in the rocks. And I don't seem to recollect it happening quite the way you're sayin'. It looked to me like Silver tried to gun the Indian down when he came out that door, but he missed, and it cost him his life. Now, do any of you have an idea where Two Bears might be headed?"

There was considerable hemming and hawing before anyone spoke up. It was one of the men he'd sat at Maggie's table with that first night, Daniel Free.

"If I was a bettin' man, which I reckon I am, I'd lay my money on him settin' his sights on the canyon yonder. He's got kin out that way. And besides, he's run off with all our money and he knows he can't show his face in Purdy again, not never."

"What do you mean by 'our money?' " said the marshal.

Free began nervously shuffling from foot to foot before he finally found the words.

"Uh, why I meant that Pearson's payroll money was in that there tin box, and that damned Two Bears took off with it."

"You ever know either one of the Pearsons to go away, then come back with a lot of money?" Kelly asked.

"No. 'Cept when they'd take some of the herd over to Purdy to sell," said Free.

"You ever go on one of these 'drives,' cowboy?"

"Why, sure, I mean that's what we're here for, ain't it?" said Free.

"Don't know. I haven't seen enough cattle around this run-down place to keep up with a payroll for two men, let alone, what, maybe ten of you?"

Free made no attempt at a response to Kelly's subtle indictment. His hand slipped dangerously close to the Colt he wore in a hand-tooled holster. He unconsciously flexed his fingers, as if he were trying to decide whether to pull his six-shooter on the marshal.

Kelly waited, too.

Chapter Eleven

Two Bears had just about ridden his mount to death as he tried to put as many miles between himself and whoever would be hunting him. He figured the town constable, Jackson, would not be able to ride for a while, if ever. By now the man could be dead for all he knew. Of course that meant a hanging when a posse caught up with him. But that was not something he intended to let happen. His aim was to get well into Black Skull Canyon, so deep into that hell-hole, in fact, that no lawman would dare poke his nose in there. "Especially that nosy marshal," he muttered to no one but his horse.

When he came to a small stream, he pulled up and jumped off his horse. He led the animal to the edge of the burbling water to drink while he moved several feet upstream to help himself to a hatful of refreshing water. His retreat from the Pearson ranch had been so hurried that he had been unable to bring anything to help him survive the harsh desert. No blankets, no food, not even a canteen. All he had to keep him going was his own determination not to get caught and strung up for shooting the constable, busting up a marshal, and to keep all of Silver's money in that tin box. That tidy pile of cash money did serve as recompense for all he'd put up with from Silver, Gold, and some of the other men at the ranch, few of whom liked having to bunk down with a half-breed Indian. And now he had all their money. The only friend Two Bears ever had at the ranch was Daniel Free, and he had no idea where Free stood at this moment after all that had happened.

It was clear he couldn't tarry long, as he was sure there would have been a posse gathered up from among the townsfolk by now, nearly all of whom had at one time or another felt a tolerable kinship with Constable Jackson. They wouldn't let his shooting go unpunished. Not for long, anyway.

As he swung into the saddle, it was getting late, with the sky growing overcast, with a promise of rain in the hills soon. That meant pushing on quickly before the dry creekbeds filled with gushing water, making crossing them treacherous, even life threatening. If he pushed hard, he could make it as far as the Barker place just on the other side of Devil's Claw, a jagged range of steep granite and sandstone cliffs that twisted around making a box canyon that all but ensured a safe haven. Besides, the Barkers were almost kinfolk. Two Bears had lived with the Barkers for a while before striking out to find a way to make better money than the pittance old man Barker paid him to help with ranch chores. Life at the Barker place had been easy for the most part, although there had been one incident in the past when bad blood had come between them, but he was certain that time had healed those old wounds and old man Barker would have forgotten the whole thing by now. At least, he hoped so, for if he was still thinking that the best thing would be a bullet to the head, his only other hope for refuge would be a hard two-day's ride further into the mountains. He was tired, hungry, and skittish about what might be on his trail and how far behind him they might be.

As the crude cabin and run-down barn and outbuildings of the Barker place came into view, he could make out a man with a rifle stepping out of the shadows of the porch. The man moved quickly toward the corral, and leaned on the top rail, resting his rifle, and aiming it directly in Two Bears' direction.

Two Bears reined in his pony, and called out.

"Mister Barker, it's me, Joseph Two Bears. You must surely remember me. I mean you no harm. I just need a place to stay for the night."

It was quickly clear that Barker had not forgotten the incident that had put up a wall between them years before.

"Stay right where you are, Two Bears, or I'll plug you where you sit. You shouldn't ought to have come back here after what you did to my Ellie."

"You never did let me explain that, Mister Barker. It wasn't my fault. We was both just young colts, and she was so pretty. If I could just talk to Ellie, I'm sure we could get back to bein' like we was before." Two Bears eased his horse forward.

Barker fired a shot that thunked into the dirt just three feet in front of Two Bear's horse. The animal shied, but Two Bears was able to keep him under reasonable control, as the horse pranced nervously for a few seconds.

"What'd you do that for? I wasn't goin' for my gun nor nothing."

"The next one'll get you for sure, you damned, low-down, murderin' snake."

Two Bears was confused by Barker's words. He hadn't ever hurt anyone that Barker would have reason to carry a grudge over. His mind was spinning, and questions flooded his search for any memory of a killing that he might have been suspect over.

"Who am I supposed to have killed? I know I've done some bad things in my life, but I ain't never killed except in self defense."

"Ellie! You killed my Ellie as sure as if you'd pulled the trigger. She's been in the ground now for almost two years, and you'll pay for it, I swear to that. Now git, or defend yourself."

The next bullet missed Two Bears' head by inches. He couldn't just let the old man gun him down, so, incensed by Barker's attitude, he yanked his rifle from its scabbard, chambered a round, and sent a shot in the old man's direction. He fired again, and again until Barker suddenly stiffened, looking like he might back off and make a run for the house. But he just stood there for a moment, straight as an arrow, his rifle dropped from his hands, and he fell hard to the ground with a bullet in his head. Two Bears' aim had been unintentionally aided by a rising wind, and, even though he had no intention of killing anyone—just wanting to make the old man quit shooting at him—the result had been fatal.

Two Bears rode to where Barker's body lay motionless in the dirt. He dismounted and leaned down. Barker's eyes were open. A trickle of blood ran down his forehead from the wound. Two Bears stood up and walked to the house hoping at least to talk Ellie into letting him have some food to take with him. He obviously couldn't stay here. As soon as someone heard about Barker, Two Bears would have even more angry men on his trail.

He came to a halt before reaching the porch. Off to his right, just beyond the house and nestled in the shadows of a cottonwood, something caught his eye. He walked over to what turned out to be a wooden marker. On it was inscribed: *Ellie Barker & unborn child. Dead at the age of 17. Killed by her own hand over a worthless man.*

Two Bears' head was reeling. He had no idea Ellie had killed herself, nor that she had been with child. Sure, he'd made some promises he hadn't yet kept, but his intentions were to come back someday and marry the girl. And maybe they should have waited till they could be married proper-like before they made love. But they were both so eager to get a taste of what marriage would bring, they lost their heads—and their better judgment. Now he knew what the old man was talking about. He could see now why Barker blamed him for the death of his only daughter. Two Bears hung his head, feeling regret for the first time in his life.

As Jed and Jake came downstairs from their hotel room the next morning, they were met in the lobby by the lanky figure of Preacher Ben Cutter. The man sauntered over to them as they reached the last step, crowding them just a little so they couldn't ignore him and walk on by.

"I understand you gents have been askin' about me. Name's Cutter, Ben Cutter. But I can't for the life of me figure out what possible interest two dudes like you could have in me." Cutter's eyes were like coal and his gaze steady and unmoving as he zeroed in on Jed.

But to Cutter's surprise, it was Jake who spoke first.

"Mister Cutter, it ain't that we got any interest in you at all, just that you looked a bit like a man we, uh, once heard about, and we was wonderin' if you was that fella. But it's clear we was wrong. We had no intention of makin' you uneasy."

"And just what was it that the fella did to made you so all fired curious?"

Now came an awkward silence from both brothers. Jake knew if they were to admit to him that he looked somewhat like one of the men who killed their brother, they'd have to admit they were gunning for him. If they lied and suggested some story that might sound good, but was untrue, would this man be able to see through their subterfuge? Jake's mouth was suddenly so dry he couldn't have worked up enough spit to make a spot on the floor. At first, Jed also stood frozen, eyes wide, and his palms moist with nervousness.

But then, out of the blue, Jed came up with an idea.

"Mister Cutter, we were just about to go in to breakfast. How about you join us and we can discuss this over a hot cup of coffee and some biscuits and gravy? We'd be honored to buy your meal, as well."

Cutter mulled the proposition over for a minute, then nodded his approval. The three of them started for the hotel dining room with Jed bringing up the rear. They seated themselves away from other customers so they wouldn't be overheard. Jed was beginning to firm up his plan and he didn't want eavesdroppers.

They ordered their food, and before Cutter could continue his line of questioning, Jed blurted out a proposal that took Jake completely by surprise.

"Mister Cutter, the truth is we are looking for some men who murdered our brother a year back. As you can tell, we surely aren't gunmen. When we heard you were in town, and found out about your reputation with a six-shooter, well, we naturally thought maybe you'd consider throwin' in with us in our quest to hunt down the rattlers that took our brother's life. That's the whole reason we were asking about you, just makin' sure we had the right fella.

"In fact, we was plannin' on makin' you a proposition once we got a chance to introduce ourselves and hear your feelings on the matter," said Jed.

Cutter sat expressionless, with no hint of being swayed by Jed's reason for following him. His stare was fixed on the saltcellar placed in the middle of the table. He slowly shifted his gaze first to Jed then to Jake. Both brothers began to perspire noticeably, as Cutter burst out in laughter. He reached over and slapped Jed on the shoulder.

"That's a good one, boys. Best I've ever heard. What's the deal?"

"Deal?" asked Jed.

"Yeah, my share of the take. You boys didn't really think I'd fall for that stupid story of yours, did you? You're lookin' for help. What is it, a train robbery, bank job, or somethin' even bigger?"

Jed and Jake looked at each other with panic in their eyes. Both men swallowed hard.

Chapter Twelve

As Kelly waited to see what the Pearson ranch hands would do next, he felt an apprehension spreading among the several men who had gathered around Silver's body. One or two of the men stepped back, turned, and began to drift toward the bunkhouse. After a few seconds another stumbled after them as if he were not certain what course to follow. The Pearson ranch's foreman called out to those who had stepped away.

"Where do you think you're going, boys?" said John Galt. "This thing ain't finished."

One man turned back and answered, "There's nothing left for us here, Galt. With Gold and Silver both dead, who's goin' to keep the ranch going? Besides, Two Bears took all the cash. Best we just move on to finding other employment. Someplace where we get paid regular instead whenever the boss gets a hankerin' to dole out that which is rightfully owed."

"You men stick around. We'll decide this thing together. Besides, the marshal here was just about to leave. Weren't you, Marshal?"

Galt's hand fell to his Colt. He gripped it as if he had every intention of drawing it should the marshal decide not to accept the thinly veiled invitation to leave. Kelly didn't move a muscle, except to slip his thumb onto the hammer of the Winchester that hung at his side. Kelly always kept a round chambered, leaving only the necessity to thumb back the hammer for it to be ready to spit out a deadly .44 caliber round. This he was prepared to do if Galt decided to follow through with his bluff. Or was it a bluff? Kelly couldn't take any chances, so he stood his ground and decided to let the chips fall where they would.

Galt watched the steely determination in the marshal's eyes. The lines had been drawn and Kelly had given him only two choices: draw or back off. If he drew, there were no guarantees that he would prove to be faster than the lawman. If he backed off, would the other men see him as a weak and inept leader? Perspiration began to form on Galt's forehead. It was rapidly becoming time for a decision. Two more of the men stepped back, holding their hands away from their holsters as a sign that they had no intention of getting involved in a gunfight with the law.

"Galt, I've heard of this marshal before. He's no

stranger to pullin' the trigger on that Winchester. If I was to guess, based on his reputation, he'll put a bullet through your gizzard before you can clear leather," said Daniel Free.

"Ain't nobody askin' you, Free. S-so shut your mouth and stay out of it," stammered Galt. While he was trying to put on a brave face, he was clearly intimidated by the cool, steady stare of the marshal.

"Sure, Galt, sure. It's your funeral." Free turned to some of the others and added, "You boys get some shovels. We'll be buryin' somethin' out back of the bunkhouse soon."

That was all it took to push Galt over the edge. He cocked the Colt as he started to draw. Kelly thumbed back the Winchester in one fluid movement and thrust the rifle into Galt's chest before Galt could clear leather, just as Free had predicted. But Kelly didn't pull the trigger and Galt just stood there, gun half out of the holster, faced with a choice that he could not win.

He wisely loosed his grip on his Colt, and let it slip back into its holster. A nervous grin crept across his grimy face. He stepped back.

"Just funnin' with you, Marshal. No harm done," Galt said, and he hastily turned to walk away.

"We aren't done here, Mister Galt," said Kelly, his rifle still raised and ready. "I have some questions that need answering before I leave."

Galt stopped. "All right, Marshal. Ask your questions and be quick about it."

"I'm looking into a murder back about a year ago up near Daleville. A man was robbed, his ranch house burned, and he was shot. There's some evidence that leads right here to this ranch, and probably to some of you. Any of you got anything to say on the matter?"

Galt frowned as he glanced around at some of the other men. Most had puzzled looks on their faces, which Kelly read as their having no knowledge of the matter or they were good actors. He just had to find out which applied.

"Just what evidence is it you're talking about, Marshal?" said Galt.

Kelly reached into his pocket and pulled out the gold watch and chain that the constable had found on Pearson's body.

"As I mentioned to Silver the last time I was out here, this handsome trinket was in Gold's possession when he was shot. It belonged to the dead man, got his name engraved right on the back. Any ideas as to where Gold got it unless he was one of the men that raided the ranch?"

"Aww, hell, Gold was always tradin' stuff. Why if a fella came to town with something Gold wanted, he'd figure out some kinda trade to get it. He probably saw that thing and thought it would make a handy time-piece. No mystery there, Marshal, everybody knew Gold liked nice things," said Galt.

"So none of you have any idea where he got it?"

"There was lots of matters that Gold and Silver

failed to divulge to us common folk," said Daniel Free. "One thing I am sure of is that neither one of the Pearsons, nor *any* of us for that matter, ever shot or robbed no one. No sir."

It was clear to Kelly that he wasn't going to get anything useful from these ranch hands. He figured he might as well get back on the trail of Two Bears. He'd sort things out after he had time to consider what he'd seen and what had been said. He touched the brim of his Stetson in mock salute and gathered up the gelding's reins.

"If any of you gents remember anything that might be useful, I'll be in town after I round up Two Bears. 'Course if he decides to tell all he knows about the matter, and I suspect he knows quite a lot, I may be forced to come back and round up any strays he might name as conspirators and haul somebody's poor, miserable carcass back for trial."

Kelly mounted up, wheeled his horse around, and started backtracking Two Bears' trail, without looking back. Galt and his men stood staring after him, each looking as if he was uncertain as to the best course to follow, whether to run or stay.

Two Bears had either been in a hurry to get all the distance he could between himself and any that had a hankering to follow, or he wasn't all that experienced at eluding posses. He had been careless about covering his trail, making tracking him about as easy as a man could hope for. Two Bears was traveling fast, pushing his horse hard, and Kelly had an idea that the half-breed would have to stop at the first ranch he could to get some of the supplies he'd be unable to gather in his haste to flee the Pearson ranch. While Kelly wasn't familiar with the ranches in the area, most were fairly easy to locate because they all had roads leading in. It was just such a meandering, dusty road that Two Bears seemed to be following, with the distance between them closing.

It was getting late in the afternoon and the skies had slowly turned an ashen grey, indicating that rain would soon be headed his way. Kelly decided that he should seek shelter soon, or risk getting drenched by a thunderstorm, possibly getting caught in rushing waters cascading down from the surrounding peaks. He'd been near dry creek beds before that suddenly became raging torrents from a thunderstorm in full fury many miles away, unseen and unheard, until a gully washer was upon you. More than one man had lost his life in just such a flood, and Kelly wasn't eager to get trapped in a similar situation this far from familiar ground. He caught sight of a trail that seemed to climb high into an outcropping of boulders, well above the narrow valley he'd been following. The rain began with a light mist that turned what had been a warm afternoon into a damp, steamy evening. While he hated to be forced to make camp and abandon Two Bears' trail, he knew it was the best decision he could make.

As he reached what looked like a good spot to bed

down, with a heavy stand of cottonwoods scattered along a struggling stream, he spotted a natural cave that would keep him dry and allow a small fire. He had no more than hobbled his gelding and gathered a few dead limbs when all hell broke loose. Thunder shook the ground as bolts of lightning lit up the nearly black sky. He scooted back as far into the cave as he could to build his fire and watch the sudden rains form instant rivers from above, gathering speed and volume as they plummeted down the steep walls of the canyon. He watched the muddy water swirl along the creek bed, bubbling as if it were brought to a furious boil. After an hour, the rain stopped as suddenly as it had started, leaving in its wake nothing more than a ghostly steam rising from sandy soil that had been forced to give up its heat by the cooling rains. Before bedding down for the night, Kelly climbed the rocks above him to get a view of the surrounding territory, perhaps to get an idea of where Two Bears might be heading.

At the top of a clutch of boulders that sat precariously along a ridge, he thought he could make out the dark shadow of a cabin, a light twinkling weakly through a small window. The trail he'd been following led straight to that cabin. He knew now where the dawn would find him as he climbed back down and settled in for the night.

Two Bears finally found a tin of matches, and scratched one across the bare table to light a lantern so he could search the cabin for valuables and supplies. The sudden storm had so darkened the sky, he had no longer been able to see inside the Barker cabin, even though he'd been there many times, both as a guest for dinner, and to meet Ellie when Barker was away. It had been one of those clandestine meetings that had brought them together in heated passion, which resulted in the events that would harden Barker's heart to Two Bears forever. For once in his life, Two Bears felt compassion for another human being, a rare emotion for one whose own upbringing had been a succession of being passed from one relative to another, beatings, hunger, and backbreaking work. By the time he was fifteen, he'd decided he'd had enough of being someone else's slave, so he lit out on his own, although not until he'd beaten a distant uncle nearly to death for spitting on him.

Seeing the way Barker had been barely scratching out a living for all these years, Two Bears could only hope he could find extra ammunition and some food he could bundle up for his trip farther back into the canyon, a trip he must hasten to make if he had any hope of eluding the posse that was certain to be hot on his trail.

After not seeing any of his family for several years, he had no idea of how he would be greeted, perhaps, with bullets, as he had been by Barker. Being a half-breed had few advantages, as he could attest to by the way he'd found himself treated by whites and Indians alike. The ranch hands at Pearson's place certainly hadn't taken to him, and the last time he saw any of his Kiowa cousins, they saw him as more of an interloper than a relative. Shunned by nearly everyone in his world, Two Bears had become a hardened, quick-tempered gunman, with few moral attributes to recommend him to society, a society that seemed to lean more toward hanging justice than to understanding and lenience. Two Bears was an outcast, and that's how he figured to end his days, which he could only hope wouldn't be any time soon.

Chapter Thirteen

"Mister Cutter, you gotta believe we, uh, didn't really have any plan for anything other than seeking justice for our poor, m-murdered brother," stammered Jake. "That's the truth, honest."

Preacher Ben Cutter stared in disbelief at the two brothers. His eyes roved back and forth from one to the other as if he couldn't decide whether to laugh at them or shoot them. Outwardly, Cutter showed no emotion, but inside, well, who knew what might be brewing beneath that ruddy complexion, those steely cold eyes, long, slightly graying hair that curled at his neck, and worn and faded denims.

Cutter didn't move a muscle for several minutes as the Bourbonette brothers squirmed in their chairs like

112

little boys awaiting a cruel stropping from their papa. The gunman was clearly aware of the discomfort he visited on others, and it was also obvious he cared not a whit for their situation, a situation he saw as of their own doing. Cutter struggled with whether to throw in with these two fools or walk away from what could be a chance at some money, something of which he was in desperate need. In fact, he was down to his last three dollars, the only remaining loot from a stagecoach hold-up he'd pulled off in Colorado months earlier.

"Suppose I was to believe this story of yours, and join your search for these supposed killers, what do I get out of it?" he said in a voice that sounded like gravel dribbling down a rocky slope.

"Why, we'd sure make it worth your while," said Jed, in obvious haste to get on the outlaw's good side.

"I want to hear the amount, and it better be substantial," said Cutter.

The word "substantial" sent a chill up Jake's spine. He had no money to speak of, and he couldn't imagine where Jed could get his hands on enough cash to make this grizzled gunman happy. They were in a serious bind, and he knew it, even if his brother seemed willing to roll the dice and risk both their lives.

"Well, uh, that's something we ain't yet settled on. What say we talk on it some and get back to you in a day or two?" said Jed.

"Sorry, boys, I ain't got a day or two to wait. Come

up with a sizable amount right now, or I'll just take outta your hides what I figure is owed me for wastin' my valuable time," said Cutter.

"Why sir, we never had no intention of wastin' the time of a man of your stature. It's just that, we, uh ain't actually thought the whole deal through yet, and wasn't quite prepared to come up with an actual figure. But, uh, I don't see why we couldn't commit to a hundred dollars for your assistance," said Jed.

"Five hundred now and another five hundred when we track down the men that shot your brother. That's the deal. Shall we shake on it?" said Cutter.

Jake was already shaking, inside, and gripping the hand of a known killer wasn't going to calm him down one bit. He knew they couldn't raise anything like that amount of money, not now, not ever. Why, he'd have to sell his store and everything in it to pay off Cutter. And he'd been gone so long now, he wasn't sure there'd be a store left when he returned. *If* he returned and *if* he could avoid getting plugged full of holes by this outlaw Jed had thought sorta fit the description of one of the men who'd robbed and burned their ranch and killed their brother. *And we figured to go up against him. What ever made me listen to my fool brother in the first place? I'm a storekeeper, not a gunman.* He was brought back to the terrifying reality of their situation by what he heard next.

"I reckon we can do business on your terms, Mister Cutter. Now, if you'll excuse me, I'll just go upstairs and get your first five hundred," said Jed, scooting his chair back and hastily rising.

"Fine. I'll just chat with your brother here while you hurry back. In case you're thinkin' of pullin' out on our deal, be assured if you come back empty-handed you'll have *another* dead brother," said Cutter.

Jake swallowed hard and broke out in a cold sweat. At least as far as he knew, there was no five hundred dollars upstairs or anywhere else for that matter. They could probably count out a hundred between them. That wouldn't be enough to spare his life.

Ben Cutter could see the fear in Jake's eyes and knew there was little chance of Jed coming back anytime soon with the money. Jed had probably conned him. Now his threats against these men had narrowed his options. If he gunned Jake down without any reason, or a chance at self-defense, he'd have to face the law or be hunted down. At least here in Arizona, thus far at least, he was not wanted for anything, and it would be foolish to end up on the run for a measly five hundred.

As ten, fifteen, then twenty minutes passed, Cutter contemplated his next move. Jake shifted nervously in his squeaky, straight-back chair, becoming more and more worried as to whether he would survive his brother's latest scheme. This wasn't the first time he'd been put in jeopardy by Jed's foolhardiness. Once, when they were sixteen, Jed devised a plan to get rich by making a plaster mold of a ten-dollar gold-piece. He then poured molten lead into the mold. After the lead cooled, he covered the counterfeit coin with gold leaf, sticking it to the surface with egg whites, in the same way it adhered to windows by sign painters. After making several of the fakes, the two of them rode over to the next town about twenty miles away and passed a coin off in exchange for merchandise from a general store. It might have worked longer if a banker hadn't noticed the coin had wrinkles where the gold leaf was not secured. It was fortunate for the boys that no one in that town knew who they were or they'd surely have been sent to prison for counterfeiting, teenagers or not. When the local sheriff heard the story, he made sure all the local merchants were on the look-out for two young boys trying to pass off fake gold pieces. That ended Jed's scheme, and it made Jake skeptical of his brother's ideas from then on.

Now he was in a dangerous situation because of Jed's misguided thinking. He was considering making a run for it, when Jed came bounding down the hotel steps. Even Cutter looked surprised at his appearance.

"Here you are, Mister Cutter, five hundred dollars, the rest to be paid on locating and disposing of the other three killers of our beloved brother," said a beaming Jed.

Cutter counted the money, folded it and stuffed it into his coat pocket.

"That's fine. Now you have to tell me what you know of these men, and where I might start looking," said Cutter.

"Uh, we'll be goin' with you so as to assure we have the right men according to the descriptions given by some folks that seen them," said Jed.

Confused by this totally unexpected turn of events, Jake nodded his shaky agreement with Jed's demand.

"Fair enough, but when the shootin' starts, you best be outta the line of fire. I'd hate for something to happen to my next five hundred."

"You don't have to worry none about that," squeaked Jake.

"Now, how about the descriptions."

For the next fifteen minutes, Jake gave Cutter a full description of the other men; just as the men who'd seen the desperadoes leaving the Bourbonette ranch the day of the killing had reported them to the sheriff of Daleville. They told him about finding Pearson down in Purdy, and explained why they had come to Tucson in search of one of the others. They also admitted that he vaguely resembled one of the men. At that, Cutter perked up as if he might know someone of that general description. He frowned, then shook his head at the thought.

"If I was a betting man, I'd say you two just described Wild Bill Hickok, who we all can attest to was shot in the back up in Deadwood in seventy-six," said Cutter.

"Don't mean there couldn't be someone else out there with the same features, does it?"

Cutter thought that over for a minute, then added,

"No, but the second one you described sure reminds me of Indian Charlie, a fella known to be hangin' out down around Tombstone, and runnin' with the Clantons, Curly Bill, and Ringo. A nasty bunch for certain."

"I ain't never laid eyes on any of the men you mentioned, so I couldn't be mistakin' one of them we're chasin' for any of them Tombstone rattlers, unless of course, one of them *is* the killer, which can't be seriously contemplated," said Jed.

Cutter stroked his chin, then pulled out a cheroot, struck a lucifer on the table leg, and lit up. He leaned back in his chair and blew a cloud of smoke in Jed's face. Jed coughed and waved away the smoke with a frown.

"All right, tomorrow we'll start our search bright and early right here in Tucson, walk every street, wander through every saloon and bordello. If they're here, we'll find them. But I've been here for nigh onto a month, and I ain't seen no one that fits your descriptions. I 'spect we'll soon be makin' tracks for Purdy to backtrack them others from where you found the one you shot."

"It happened a year ago, so I doubt they hung around the same place for long," said Jake.

"Yep, you're right. But folks remember when they meet up with hombres like the ones you've described. We'll find 'em."

Cutter got up and strode to the front door and outside

without another word. As soon as he left, Jake let out a sigh of relief.

"You scared the hell outta me, Jed. I could shoot you myself. Where'd you find all that money?"

"Don't you worry none about that right now. I'll take care of the money end of things; you can count on it. And we won't have to come up with no more for that hombre, neither. In fact, I checked with the sheriff. Cutter is wanted in Colorado and there's a reward of one thousand dollars on his head. When the time comes, we'll get our brother's killers and make a nice profit, too."

"Are you plumb outta your mind? You're gonna get us killed with your schemes one of these days," said Jake, shaking his head in disbelief at Jed's words.

Just then, the Bourbonettes heard a ruckus out on the street. Jake jumped from his chair and ran to the door to see what the fuss was all about. The owner of the general store next to the hotel was shouting he'd been robbed. Sheriff Smith and a deputy were running toward him.

"Sheriff, I been busted into and robbed. Took all my cash while I was outside sweepin' the boardwalk. I never even heard a sound."

"Calm down, George, we'll get to the bottom of this. Now show me where the robbin' took place."

Jake went outside to follow the crowd that had begun to gather in front of the store. After a couple of minutes, the sheriff came back outside and addressed the onlookers.

"George, here, was robbed sometime earlier this mornin' whilst he was working outside. Someone must have snuck in the back way and busted open his cash drawer. Took it all. Now if anybody saw anything suspicious goin' on in the alley out back, I'd be obliged if you'd come by the jail and tell me what you know."

"There goin' to be a reward, Sheriff?" asked one of the gawkers.

"That'd be up to the owner. How about it, George? Did the thief get away with enough to make offerin' a reward practical?"

"Uh, well, I reckon I could come up with twenty-five dollars." He reached into his pocket and withdrew a fold of bills.

"Aww, hell, George, that ain't 'nough to get a good buzz on," said one of the men in the crowd. A titter went through those gathered behind him.

"Sorry, but they took every last bit I had, five hundred dollars!"

Chapter Fourteen

As false dawn broke over the Barker homestead, Two Bears bundled up what supplies he'd managed to steal and checked his six-shooter to be sure he'd replenished his supply of cartridges before leaving the cabin. *It's too damned bad I can't just stay and take this place over. Barker had no relatives and I wouldn't have to put up with no one lookin' at me like I was poison or something*, he thought. He'd stuffed a gunnysack with all the canned goods he could find. It was heavy, so he half-carried, half-dragged it to the door.

As he stepped from the doorway, he heard the distinctive click of a hammer being cocked and felt the cold steel of a rifle barrel jammed against his cheek. His eyes grew as big as silver dollars as he froze mid-step.

"Make a move for that Colt, Two Bears, and the last

thing you'll hear in this world is the sound of my voice," said Kelly. "Drop that sack and slowly unbuckle your gun belt."

Two Bears shivered as he did as the voice demanded. He knew he had no choice. He was out of options. He silently berated himself for not leaving in the night, even though he had no doubt he was being pursued, possibly by a whole posse, and they wouldn't be far behind. His gun and holster dropped onto the porch floor with a thud. The gunnysack hit the porch like an anvil. He slowly lifted his hands and turned slightly to see who had the drop on him. A defeated grin crawled across his face when he saw the badge.

"Sorry about that lump on your head, Marshal. I don't know what I was thinkin' when I cracked you a good one back in Purdy. Reckon I was a little drunk when I plugged the constable too. I didn't kill him, did I?"

"No. He'll live, but I reckon you're goin' to spend a while behind bars."

"Damn. I swear if I didn't have bad luck, I'd have no luck at all," said Two Bears.

"Luck didn't have anything to do with me trackin' you down. You're about the worst owlhoot on the scout as any I've seen for a spell."

"Yeah. I never spent enough time with my Kiowa cousins to learn their ways."

"Maybe if you'd quit doin' stupid things, folks wouldn't be tracking you down."

"How'd you find me?"

"I'm a fair tracker and, like I said, you're pretty easy prey. Now, you're going to put on these shackles and then you're going to bury that man lying out there by the corral. Too bad you had to shoot an innocent man just for some tins of beans. That'll probably make things go worse for you at trial."

Two Bears screwed up his face, looking for sympathy. "He wasn't so innocent. He shot at me first. I was only defendin' myself. Check his rifle. You'll see I'm tellin' the truth." He looked down at the ground, shaking his head. "I had no damned choice. None."

After checking Two Bears' story and finding spent cartridges lying near where the man had fallen, Kelly went to find something the bury the corpse with. He found a rusty shovel leaning against a shed and handed it to Two Bears. "Start diggin'."

"With that Winchester pointed at me, I reckon I don't have a choice," Two Bears said.

"Nope."

Just then Two Bears made a move that was too slow and too obvious. He slid the shovel just under the top layer of dirt and gravel, then quickly shifted his weight as he yanked up hard to throw the dirt in the marshal's face. But Kelly saw it coming and spun away just in time. The dirt missed, but Two Bears quickly shifted his weight and he started to swing the shovel down on the marshal. A rifle shot that blew up dirt between his feet convinced the half-breed to stop mid-swing. He sighed as he eased the shovel to the ground.

"Try something like that again and I'll be takin' you back across your saddle. Now get that hole dug with no more trouble or I might start thinkin' real serious-like of saving the county the cost of a trial."

Two Bears dug, although not without considerable grumbling. The rocky ground was hard-packed and dry, despite the rain that had fallen furiously for a short time the night before. When the hole was sufficiently deep, the two of them dropped Barker's body into it, and began to cover it up.

"Just curious, what made you come here in the first place? I figured you'd head straight for the canyon," said Kelly.

"I once worked for old man Barker here on this place. Wasn't much of a job, mostly muckin' out the barn or chasin' scrawny cattle through the brush. I only stayed because I was sweet on his daughter, even thought maybe there could be a future with her. But he'd hear none of it. 'No half-breed is gonna be grabbin' his filthy hands onto this family tree,' he said. So, one day I took spurs to my pony and disappeared."

"I noticed a grave out back for a girl named Ellie. That have anything to do with you?"

"When I rode in yesterday, Barker started yellin' that I killed her. That's when he begun blastin' away at me. I didn't even know she was dead, nor anything about a baby. I reckon I came by to see her more than anything else. I had no idea she'd killed herself over the likes of me."

Kelly saw pain in the man's eyes and decided not to press him further about the girl. Perhaps for the first time in his forlorn life the truth had passed Two Bears' lips.

Before Two Bears could push too hard to get sympathy from the marshal, Kelly walked to Two Bears' horse, removed his rifle from its scabbard and untied the tin box from the leather straps that held it to the cantle. He carried both the rifle and the tin to his own black gelding, stuffing the box into a saddlebag.

"I'll just take charge of Mister Pearson's bank for the time bein', at least until we get to town. Best saddle up. We got a long ways to go."

As they slowly retraced the route Two Bears had taken to Barker's ranch, Kelly remained silent for the first hour. Two Bears could be important to him if he was ever to find out what part the Pearsons may have played in the death of Albert Bourbonette. But since getting him to open up might put him in more trouble than he was already in, the marshal decided to wait until Two Bears decided talking might get him a better deal. While shooting a peace officer was going to land Two Bears in jail for certain, shooting down Silver Pearson and robbing him would depend on any testimony the ranch hands might be willing to give. Killing Barker would be tough to prove as anything other than self-defense, since the dead man did have a rifle lying beside him with several shots fired. Two Bears could get a hanging sentence for that only if it could be proven he went there with the intent to kill Barker. Kelly doubted that.

The marshal pondered how best to go about getting information without Two Bears going completely silent, perhaps all the way to his grave. At this point, Two Bears was the only connection he had that could lead him to the Bourbonette murder. Kelly knew he had to stretch out the time it took to get his prisoner back to Purdy. Spotting a grassy patch under a stand of willows, he reined in.

"We'll stop here for awhile, Two Bears. Get down off your mount and head for those trees yonder, by the creek," said Kelly.

Two Bears did as he was told. He led his bay to the creek, which still had a trickle of water flowing aimlessly down the center from the previous evening's rainfall. He dropped the reins and fell into the tall grass. His hands were secured by the iron shackles Kelly had put on him, so he could do little more than lie there in the shade awaiting his next order from a marshal he assumed would just as soon shoot him as haul him all the way back to town. Kelly's next words brought a puzzled look to his dark face.

"Look around and see what you can find to build a fire, Two Bears, so we can get some coffee going. I've got a can of beans we can heat up, too."

Is this marshal crazy? How can he not know I'll try to make a run for it when I get a little ways away from the campsite? Why would he trust me, especially when I whacked him over the head after shooting the constable? Two Bears slowly struggled to his feet and wandered off, keeping his head low so the marshal would think he was looking for wood instead of what he was actually doing, silently questioning the lawman's actions, as well as waiting for the perfect opportunity to escape.

Willows drop lots of thin, useless twigs, and they lay scattered about like thatch. That would make good tinder to start a fire, but would burn so quickly as to be useless to cook over. Two Bears was hungry enough to eat about anything, so he hunted for any fallen limbs that might burn long enough to heat up those beans the marshal had mentioned. He stumbled over the long dead remains of a fallen juniper, and began breaking it into smaller pieces across his knee. The wood was hard but would make a nice, hot fire. He lugged several pieces back to the campsite. The marshal had hobbled both of their mounts and was seated with his back to the approaching half-breed, as if unconcerned that a man who had proven to be hostile could come upon him from the rear and take another crack at him. *Is this the time to make a break for it?*

Without turning, Kelly spoke with a deep, authoritative voice. "If you're contemplating making a break for it, I'd reconsider, Two Bears."

"Uh, not me, Marshal. I did just what you told me, got wood."

"Good. Bring it over here and dump it in the center of these rocks."

Two Bears placed the twigs on the bottom and the

heavier limbs on top, then gathered some dried grass to help get the fire started. Kelly struck a sulfur and put it to the dry grass. The flame caught immediately. In minutes they had a fire sufficient to make coffee and heat up a tin of beans. While they were eating, Kelly began to casually question Two Bears about his employment at the Pearson ranch.

"How long have you been working for the Pearsons?"

"About a year and a half. Wasn't much of an outfit, though." He mumbled as he scooped up beans like he hadn't eaten for a month.

"Just how did they manage to make enough money to pay all the hands? It didn't look like they had enough livestock to keep two men busy, let alone almost a dozen. Can you explain that?"

Two Bears tried not to look up, knowing that if he did the marshal might see he wasn't telling the truth. "Nope. I sure can't say. Never did have much of a head for the business end of ranching."

"Doesn't take a school teacher to figure out that a dozen cattle scattered across five hundred acres of scrubby desert don't add up to a herd needin' all those men. What I want from you is the truth. Just how did the Pearsons get enough money to pay all you hands?"

Two Bears was caught between playing ignorant, risking the full penalty for robbery and murder, or telling the truth and maybe using that to get a lighter sentence. Or, if he was lucky, maybe no sentence at all. His dark-eyed, youthful expression begged for understanding.

"Would you be willin' to go easy on me if I was to tell you what you want to know?"

Chapter Fifteen

Jake was stunned by the store owner's claim that he had been robbed of exactly five hundred dollars, the very amount Jed had given Ben Cutter as a down payment on his agreeing to help track down the killers of their brother. As the crowd gathering in the street grew more restless, the sheriff told everyone to go back to whatever they were doing and leave the town's policing duties to him and his deputy. Although the heat of day already had a firm grip on the thermometer, Jake felt a chill as he went inside to find Jed seated at a table near the window, as always, with a deck of cards in his hand.

"Jed, did you hear what that storeowner said?" Jake's demeanor was clearly that of a man who was trying to do a dance between anger and panic.

"Nope. Wasn't listenin', brother. Was it important?"

"Yeah, maybe. Especially if his claim of being robbed wasn't just a coincidence. He said it had happened just a few minutes ago. Where'd you manage to lay your hands on five hundred dollars so quickly? And what the hell took you so long when you went upstairs, leavin' me alone with that stone cold killer?"

"Whatever's got your britches afire? I wasn't gone but a minute or two. I just needed to go through all my things to locate the right amount of cash. I sorta keep it spread out over several pockets and hidey-holes. I've never been keen on leaving it all in one place for some sneak thief to latch onto. A soul can't be too careful these days, you know?"

"You expect me to believe you had that much money just tucked away?"

"Don't much care what you believe. It's the truth. Have I ever lied to you before?"

Jake just stood there, dazed, shaking his head and breathing hard.

"How would I know if you had? We ain't seen each other for over a year, since before Albert was killed. Sometimes I'm not sure who you really are, Jed. You do crazy things."

"I'm your brother, Jake, blood kin, and you ought not to forget that. Why, I can't tell you how disappointed I am at hearin' even a note of disparagement about me in your voice. I am cut deeply by your lack of faith."

"Uh-huh. Well, if that sheriff takes it into his head to come lookin' for whoever latched onto that man's five hundred dollars, and he takes a notion to talk to Preacher Ben Cutter, I'm bettin' Cutter will sell you out quicker'n a jilted hussy. You better not be lying to me, 'cause if you are, we could both be tuggin' on a piece of hemp."

Jed got up and came over to Jake. He put his hand on Jake's shoulder.

"Listen, Jake, I didn't take nobody's money. Won it fair and square from folks who weren't quite as good with the pasteboards as me, that's all. And that's the truth. Now put the whole thing out of your mind. They got nothing that could suggest I had anything to do with the robbery."

Jake turned in a huff and stomped up the stairs to their room. Jed could tell that his last words had done nothing to calm his brother's concerns over the source of the five hundred dollars.

Once inside their room, Jake walked to the window, parted the curtain, and stared down on the street. Wagons and buggies rattled by, people criss-crossed the rutted roadway, and horses shook their heads and shifted their stance at the hitching rails. Somewhere a dog barked at the heels of a pair of mules pulling a supply wagon down an alley. The smells of cooking wafted up into the room, mixing with the dust from the street traffic and the foul aroma of dung. His trust in whatever his brother said appeared to be waning, and that wasn't the way brothers should feel toward each other.

Jake thought back to when a Chiricahua raiding party killed their parents ten years ago. Their brother, Albert, had been the only one willing to stay and try to make the ranch work. Jed had never liked working cattle and struck out on his own just as soon as he had enough money to get him to someplace where games of chance were aplenty. Jed's knack for gambling and other sorts of risk-taking hadn't changed, and probably never would, at least to Jake's way of thinking. But then, he too had never had a love for ranching, and he, like his brother, Jed, sold his share of the Bourbonette holdings to Albert. The only difference was, he wanted the money to start a business in town, something less risky than getting stomped in the dirt by stampeding cattle, outlasting the droughts, and finding a reliable market for their beef. Albert had borrowed up to the hilt to buy his brothers out.

Jake remembered how the ranch seemed to thrive under Albert's guidance, at least at first. He had been hardworking, resourceful, appeared to like being his own boss, and had always been at home around livestock. Albert had let it be known that the idea of sharing responsibility for the ranch's operations didn't sit well with him, and that's why he'd jumped at the chance to be shed of two brothers who didn't show any real tendency toward hard work. Albert was a hardworking active man, who had often told his brothers that he hoped someday to find a woman who would share his love of the range and settle down with him.

The day Sheriff John Wilmont burst into Jake's store in Daleville to tell him there had been a shooting at his brother's ranch, Jake insisted on accompanying the posse. When they arrived, Jake remembered seeing every building burned to the ground. His brother's body lay on the grass under a tree. No weapon was found nearby. He told the sheriff he couldn't believe his eyes. Who would put a bullet in an unarmed man? And why? He told the sheriff that as far as he knew, Albert had no money to speak of. All of his assets had been tied-up in building the herd, most of which he'd sold off just prior to the robbery. The bank still held a large note against the ranch.

As he stared out at the people in the street below, Jake's mind raced back to that day, and the sight of seeing his brother sprawled out like a rag doll on the ground, a splotch of blood covering his shirt. He remembered leaning down, half-expecting him to awaken like nothing had happened. He was still visibly shaken at the funeral. He had tried to find his brother, Jed, but had no idea where to start the search. Jed hadn't kept in touch for months. And now Jake was wondering what suddenly brought Jed out of the woodwork and into his life again. Where had he been all that time? Had he been in some sort of trouble? Then one day, out of nowhere, his brother strode into his store on a Saturday afternoon, pretty as you please, with no explanation of his long absence, and announced that he had come back for a visit.

Jake was pacing the floor nervously when Jed opened the door to their room.

Jed could see that Jake hadn't bought into his denial at stealing money to give to Cutter. He had to do or say something to smooth things over. Jumpy people make mistakes. All too often they shoot off their mouth in front of the wrong person and stir up a whole hornet's nest of trouble. And Jed knew he could be on the receiving end of that trouble. He looked over at Jake's suitcase lying open across the bed, and he quickly picked up on Jake's struggle with what to do.

"Now, Jake, you got to listen to me, and forget that storeowner. We're on an important mission here to find our dear brother's killers, and we can't let anything stand in the way of that. What we have to do is follow the plan. Cutter will be here first thing in the morning and we better be ready. He don't strike me as a patient man, so if we're gonna get our money's worth outta him, we have to be together on this."

While Jake was still silently fuming inside at his brother's cavalier attitude toward involving a known gunman in their quest, he nevertheless held a strange admiration for Jed's nerve. But his continuing suspicions about whether his brother had slipped in the back door of the dry goods store and stolen the owner's money while leaving *him* at the mercy of Ben Cutter, clung to him like mud on a new pair of boots. He felt as if he had no control over his own destiny. He was dubious about riding alongside a known killer and a brother who kept secrets as if they were no more than a few extra handkerchiefs. A decision had to be made. Once resigned to his fate, he turned to Jed.

"All right, Jed, I'll put my trust in your story just this one time, but I warn you, if I find out you've lied to me, don't count me as your brother no more. And if the law comes courtin' you, don't be lookin' to me to bail you out. You understand?"

"You'll not be sorry, brother. I'll not let you down. After all, how could kin betray kin?"

"That's a good question," said Jake.

The next morning, a good night's sleep seemed to have smoothed out most of the rancor that had buzzed between them the day before. "Come on, then, it's almost time to meet Cutter and get started after those scoundrels," said Jed.

With that, they left their room and headed outside to find Ben Cutter. They didn't have to wait long.

"Well, boys, I reckon you'll be wantin' to begin your search for them elusive devils that killed your brother. Let's get at it, then."

"What's your suggestion for how we start, Mister Cutter?"

"Listen, boys, since we're goin' to be workin' together real close, why don't you get used to just callin' me Ben. And, as far as the how of this operation, well I'd say we need to sit down and go over everything you know of the descriptions you got from the sheriff in Daleville once more."

"Fair 'nough," said Jed. They walked to a bench outside of City Hall and Jed commenced to tell what he'd been told by Sheriff Wilmont in Daleville when he came back to town and was informed of his brother's murder. Jake provided additional information.

The brothers frowned at each other's comments every once in a while, but neither interrupted the other. Jed's problem was that the sheriff had relayed to him some details that were different from Jake's telling. When his brother finished, Jed had a few questions of his own, and a slightly different sequence of events.

"Jake, I don't mean to quarrel with what you said, but there seems to be some discrepancies that need to be ironed out. First off, the sheriff told me that them folks said they saw four men leaving the ranch house in a hurry, but didn't actually see anyone shoot Albert," said Jed.

"If they didn't, then who could have? That's a small detail as I see it," said Jake.

"Maybe, maybe not. By the time he got out there, a lot could have happened. The sheriff told me that a rider from the next ranch saw smoke and rode over to see what was goin' on. He's the one that found Albert lying there, dead and then rode into town to report it. The sheriff hadn't heard from them other folks until the next day, after he got back to town, and they came by to report that they'd seen four men riding away from the ranch," said Jed.

"Hold up, here. Who saw what don't amount to a stack of cow pies, as I see it. If someone got a gander at them four, that's good enough for me. I say we get to the task at hand, and bag ourselves some coyotes," said Cutter. "And heaven help 'em when we do."

Chapter Sixteen

Kelly was about to pour more coffee into Two Bears' cup when the pot was blown out of his hand by a bullet slamming into it. The shot sent the tin pot skittering across the rocks and the two of them diving for cover. The blast reached their ears, echoing through the boulders a split second after Kelly hit the dirt. He drew his Colt, raised his head slightly, and glanced around quickly to see if he could see any remnants of smoke indicating where the shot might have come from.

A second bullet dug into the ground inches from where Kelly lay. He rolled away, scooting behind some rocks for cover. A third shot thudded into something nearby. He looked around and saw Two Bears still in the open.

"Two Bears, can you crawl over here?"

"I-I'm hit. I can't move my leg. It hurts bad."

Kelly stuck his head up, then ducked back as another bullet ricocheted off a boulder two feet away. He threw a couple of shots in the direction he thought the firing was coming from, hoping it would give him a chance to grab Two Bears and pull him to cover. But as soon as he started to move another couple of bullets thudded into the ground nearby, too close to let him leave the security of his position. He was unable to identify anything more than the general direction of the gunfire.

Two Bears struggled to scoot and crawl toward the marshal. Bullets kicked up dirt all around him. When he was within three feet, Kelly dove for him and yanked him out of the line of fire, tugging him into a depression under the rocky outcropping. More shots, none coming close enough for worry, ricocheted off rocks and dug into trees. He saw a splash of blood on Two Bears' denims. He pulled off his neckerchief and tied it tightly around the wound to stop the bleeding.

"How bad is it?"

"Hurts like fire, but I don't think it hit the bone," said Two Bears.

"You get a chance to see where the shooter is?"

"I'm bettin' it's coming from across that ravine, probably on top of the ridge there to the right. Looks like the only place where they could keep us pinned down."

"If you're right, then this Colt might as well be a slingshot. I need to get to my rifle."

"You'll be puttin' yourself right in the line of fire. If you get shot, what chance do I have? These shackles don't even give a man any chance to defend himself. How about at least givin' me my six-shooter? I could cover you while you make a try for your Winchester. Whadda you say?"

"I'd say you been smokin' peyote."

"Well, then call that horse of yours over here and grab that rifle. Send some lead back their way so's we got a chance." He tried to get to his knees.

"I'm not aiming to get my horse shot. Now why don't you just settle down and let me work this out. And keep your head down unless you think a couple extra holes in it might improve your judgment."

Two Bears fell back onto the grass, moaning and groaning, grumbling something about nobody giving a damn about what happens to a poor half-breed. Kelly just shook his head as he glanced about for some solution to their predicament.

The first thoughts to strike him were concerning who would be most interested in their demise. As far as he knew, he'd made no enemies in Purdy, which lay about eight miles from where they were hunkered down behind the outcropping of boulders. Then, it hit him. The obviousness of it now became disgustingly clear. Galt and some of the boys from the Pearson ranch must have been lying in wait for them to return to Purdy, fig-uring Kelly would locate Two Bears and at least try to bring him out alive. Since that's exactly what he'd done, the Pearson bunch wanted their money back, and probably Two Bears' life in exchange for their leader.

"Sure as hell wish I knew who had it in for us. Probably some fool figurin' to rob us," said Two Bears.

"I doubt that. I figure it's some of your old friends out there lookin' for a little revenge. How many of them would side with Galt to ambush a marshal?"

"Well, the two you gunned down earlier were pretty loyal to Silver, although they were both dumber than a sack of month-old manure. Now, with Silver gone, Galt can probably only count on Daniel Free and maybe one or two more. The others'll scatter now that they ain't got any hope of getting' paid for their measly chores. At least they were gettin' fed while Silver was alive. Maybe I shouldn't have plugged him, just grazed the crazy coyote."

"It's a little late to be thinking' about what you should have done."

"Yeah, I 'spect. Somehow, I always seem to come up with answers long after the question done come and gone. My whole life has been one mistake after another."

Kelly was only half-listening to the breed's self-indulgent meanderings. He was busy working up a plan of escape. The risk was high, but, if it worked, they would be clear of the threat of being gunned down while they hid behind a bunch of rocks. He looked over at Two Bears, who was now pushed so far back beneath the boulder overhang it would take a logging chain to pull him out.

"Listen. I'm going to make a break for it, and you're going to stay right here. I can't get away with you taggin' along all crippled up. So, whatever you do, keep snug under that overhang where you'll be safe. They probably won't come for you until they're sure you ain't packin'."

"You can't just up and leave me here alone with no way to defend myself. Why, when they figure out you're gone and I'm still here, I'll be no more than snake bait. Leave me my pistol, at least."

"Nope. You might just take it into your mind to shoot yourself, or worse, me if I make it back. Now shut up and relax."

Kelly jumped up and started racing for where his horse stood hobbled under some trees. He tried to stay as low as possible, weaving and dodging to make a more difficult target. After several shots rang out, most thudding into the ground behind him, one ripped through his shirt and vest. A searing pain in his side knocked him off his feet as a bullet grazed him, digging a bloody furrow in his flesh. Fortunately, his momentum carried him several feet further into some tall grass where he was hidden temporarily from the shooter. He gasped for breath, then struggled to his feet and, staying as low as possible, kept going until collapsing just on the other side of a little rise where he was out of the line of sight of the man with a rifle.

He rolled over to examine where and how seriously he'd been hit. *Feels like it just grazed a rib, probably cracked it, but the bullet don't seem to still be in there. That's a piece of luck.* He pulled a handkerchief from his back pocket and stuffed it in his shirt to help stem the stream of blood flowing down his side.

He crawled to where his horse was still grazing unconcerned with the shots echoing through the valley, and safely out of the line of fire. He freed the gelding from its restraints, then pulled himself up by the stirrup, and got mounted. He yanked his rifle from its scabbard, and kicked the animal to a run, in the opposite direction from where Two Bears was huddled, making no attempt to keep his escape secret. He heard shouts from Two Bears as he rode away.

"Hey, you can't leave me here. Damn you, lawman. I'll kill you if I get out of this!"

Kelly kept riding until he came to a split in the creek. There was a deer trail that circled around, leading up and over a ridge that looked down on the grassy area where he and his captive had made camp. As he reached the top, he could easily make out where the shots had been coming from. He dismounted, pulled his field glasses from his saddlebag and squatted behind some brush to await the ambushers' next move. He could clearly make out at least two of the gunmen, and one was definitely Galt. He didn't have to wait long for them to make their intentions known.

Four men slowly emerged from behind some rocks directly across the ravine from where Kelly had chosen to camp. The shooters had a perfect vantage point from which to keep their quarry pinned down. They were cautious as they slipped from behind their cover. Kelly watched as three of the men began to ease down the slope from where they'd been well-hidden by thick brush and mesquite. The fourth man, Galt, stayed behind to cover their descent. They slowly made their way in the direction of where Two Bears was hiding. When they were about three hundred yards away, Kelly made his next move.

Pressing his left hand to his wound to keep the blood loss to a minimum as he climbed down from the rocks, Kelly slipped and slid down the steep, gravel-covered hillock. If he had figured correctly, when he reached the bottom, he would be between Galt and the others, positioned behind the three who had obviously been sent to find Two Bears and send him on his way to oblivion. The marshal had no intention of letting that happen. With his Winchester tightly clutched in his right hand, and using it for balance, he came to a sliding stop against a fallen tree. He began trotting toward the spot he'd picked as the best place for a stand against the bushwhackers.

As Kelly climbed between two boulders, he saw

what he had hoped to see—three men advancing on Two Bears, completely out in the open. His own position kept him out of sight of Galt. He took aim on the first of the three, and fired. The man dropped before the others could identify where the shot had come from. The second man went down as he was trying to reach cover behind a plume of prickly pear cactus. The third man dove behind some rocks and started sprinting back towards Galt's position. As Kelly moved forward to see if either of the men he'd shot was still alive, he could hear the echoing thuds of horses charging away as if the devil himself was on their heels.

After returning to their camp and helping Two Bears to his feet, Kelly led him to where the two dead men lay.

"Were these men employed by the Pearsons?"

"That one over there is Pritchard. The other one just came last week. I didn't even know his name. Did you get a peek at the other two?"

"Galt and Daniel Free, I suspect. Didn't get a real good look at anyone but Galt."

"Well, you saved our necks, Marshal. Reckon you can haul me into town now where they'll want to stretch mine."

"It don't pay to start pullin' dirt in on yourself just yet. This thing's got a ways to go before it's all sorted out. I figure you still got answers I need concerning a man's death, and I'll not let anything happen to you until you open up."

"I don't know nothin' about no man gettin' killed."

"Maybe, maybe not. Before I'm finished with you I intend to know everything you know about that Pearson bunch. And if you keep holdin' out on me, I'll string you up myself," said Kelly. He lead Two Bears by the arm and helped him onto his horse, then took the reins and walked him to where he'd left his black gelding.

"I see you seem to have sprung a leak yourself, Marshal. I sure do hope you can make it back to Purdy without fallin' outta the saddle from loss of blood. That'd just be a damned shame."

Chapter Seventeen

After spending nearly a day wandering the streets of Tucson with no luck in spotting anyone remotely resembling Albert's killers, Jake and Jed had finally agreed with Cutter that the logical thing to do was to leave Tucson, ride back to Purdy and start from where they had shot Gold Pearson. As they prepared to saddle up, Cutter pushed the brothers for more information about the killers.

"Tell me again how you found out about this fella you shot."

"I heard that he fit the description of one of the men that was seen at the ranch that day," said Jake.

"Who told you about him?" said Cutter.

"It's been a while back. I don't rightly remember his name. But he sounded real sure of his claim."

"Say, when we ride into Purdy, that constable ain't goin' to be lookin' to string you two fellas up, is he? And maybe anyone else you happen to have taken up with?"

"Nope. He never even sent a posse out after us. Musta been satisfied it was self-defense, so, I reckon we're free to come and go as we please," said Jed, with a self-satisfied grin.

"What about the man you shot, anyway? What was his name? Did he have friends that might consider a little revenge as your proper comeuppance?"

"We don't know anything about the man. Never did get his name, or even where he lived. Nothin'. Just that he could be found in Purdy, probably at the gamblin' tables," Jake said.

"Now let me get this straight. Are you sayin' you just sauntered into this saloon, walked over to a stranger and plugged him without makin' sure he was your man?" said Cutter, with a doubting frown on his weathered face.

Even a man like Preacher Ben Cutter, with a reputation for never hesitating to use a Colt to settle his differences, was feeling ill at ease with the boy's explanation of the sequence of events. Something about the whole thing smelled like something that should have buzzards circling above it. He had his five hundred, and that should have been sufficient, but the more he learned, the less confidence he had in the whole story. Maybe his desperate need for cash had made him soft in the head, he thought. It drifted through his confused mind that it might all just be a trick to catch him off-guard, maybe stick a gun in his gut, and haul him in for the reward that was on his head in Colorado. He squinted hard as he looked over at Jake, and then at Jed. He shook his head, muttering something under his breath that sounded an awful lot like, "Naw, they probably are just what they seem, a couple of tinhorns out to get someone else to do their dirty work."

"He fit the description, sure enough. Right down to the way his belly drooped over his belt like a sack of flour strung up too tight. Eyes too close together, more like a snake than a man. And that big nose of his had a bend in it like he'd slipped and fell on his face, and it just stayed folded over. Nope, there weren't no doubt about him bein' the right man, not in my mind, anyway," said Jed.

"Them passersby must have got right friendly with them killers to come up with a description with them kind of details," said Cutter, shaking his head. He reached into his shirt pocket and drew out a plug of tobacco. He bit off a hunk, then offered some to the others. Both shook their heads. Jake made a face that suggested he'd rather take a beating than chew tobacco.

Cutter took off his hat, ran his fingers through his long, oily hair, then replaced it low on his forehead, the brim nearly covering his eyes. "All right boys, let's hit the trail for Purdy," he said as he swung into the saddle. The three rode down the dusty streets of Tucson and out into the desert to the southeast, toward the mountains, and a showdown.

They hadn't ridden far when a dust cloud appeared behind them. Four horses were coming fast. The trio stopped and waited for the riders to catch up to them.

"Be ready to defend yourselves if this bunch is aimin' on a hold-up or somethin'," said Cutter. The brothers sat quietly.

"It's Sheriff Smith," said Jake. "Looks like his tail feathers are on fire."

As the four riders reached Cutter and the Bourbonette brothers, the sheriff held up short in front of Jed.

"Sorry boys, but I got to check you out before you get too far away. Someone robbed the drygoods store this mornin', and I just got a hankerin' to make sure you three didn't have nothin' to do with it. Hope you don't mind showin' me what's in your pockets."

Jed spoke first. "You're welcome to search me, Sheriff. Check my pockets and my saddlebags, too, if you've a mind to. I got nothin' to hide."

"Same here," said Jake. "I'm down to about thirty dollars to my name, anyway."

The sheriff followed through with his search of the brothers, then stopped before checking Cutter. The look on his face said he shouldn't push this man too far or risk ending up pushing up daisies on some dusty hillside graveyard. He stopped, cocked his head, then said, "Hmmm. I seem to recollect I saw you sitting out front of the hotel about the time the robbery occurred, Cutter. Reckon you couldn't have had anything to do with it."

He went back to his horse and mounted up.

"Hope I didn't inconvenience you fellas none. Have a good trip." The sheriff and his posse wheeled their horses about and headed back in the direction of town. They were out of sight before anyone spoke.

"That was a close one, boys. Good thing he didn't open up them saddlebags of mine, wasn't it, Jed?" said Cutter.

"Uh, I don't know what you mean. That five hundred I gave you wasn't stolen."

Cutter looked amused. "Uh-huh."

It was late in the day when they reached Purdy. Cutter led the boys to the saloon, which, he insisted, was as good a place as any to start their search by washing the grit out of their mouths with whiskey. Plenty of whiskey. "A man can't ask questions if his throat is so clogged with desert he can't speak without raisin' a dust."

"You two go ahead. I think I'll find us a place to bed down," said Jake. He rode on down the street to locate a hotel or boarding house with a vacancy. When he came to the hotel, he dismounted and stepped onto the plank walkway, pushed open the door, and went inside to find a smallish man with a great shock of white hair leaning on the counter, poring over what appeared to be the hotel's registry.

"Howdy. I'm looking for a room for three. Probably need it for a couple of nights. Name's Jake, Jake Bourbonette."

The man slowly looked up, pushed his spectacles up on his nose and squinted at Jake.

"I know who you are. Seen you before. Didn't catch your name that time, but I never forget a face. You were with the fella that shot and killed Gold Pearson. I was in the saloon that day."

"Gold Pearson?"

"That was his name. Reckon you was in too much of a hurry to put a bullet in him to ask who he was. Around here, we generally get to know a fella for a few minutes before we start blastin' away at him."

"It wasn't like that. He drew on my brother, first. He didn't deserve to live."

"Hmmm. Not many of us do, nowadays."

"What do you mean by that?" Jake said.

"Oh, nothin' in particular," said the desk clerk. "Now, how many did you say would be stayin'?"

"Three of us. Won't be for long."

"Well, just sign the register. That's gonna be four bits for each night you hang around, although I'd suggest you don't stay too long."

"Why do you say that?"

"Well, the way I hear it, the boys out at the Pearson ranch ain't takin' too kindly to them that's killed one of their bosses."

"Bosses?"

"Yep. Gold and Silver Pearson. Twin brothers. Their own mother couldn't tell 'em apart. Figured you knowed that."

Jake hastily dropped several coins on the desk, signed the register in a flurry of scribbles, and rushed out the door to find Jed. He found his brother leaning on the bar with a beer in his hand. Cutter was nearby talking to some rough-looking cowboys at a table. Jake tried signaling to his brother to come outside without Cutter tagging along, but was unable to get his attention away from a bartender who had apparently intrigued him with some tall tale, as Jed was laughing intermittently as the man gestured wildly. Finally, in desperation, he walked up behind Jed, grabbed him by the shoulder and jerked his head toward the door, suggesting his brother should follow him.

"Wh-what's the matter, Jake? Can't a fella take time to slake a thirst?"

Jake had a deep frown on his face as he whispered for his brother to follow him outside. Jed complied with a shrug and a shake of his head as if to say, "What could possibly be so damned important?" Cutter didn't seem to take notice of their leaving.

When they got to the plank walk, Jake grabbed his brother's arm and tugged him hard. There was fear in his eyes. He shook as he spoke, keeping his voice low, but leaving no doubt as to there be something serious to talk over.

"Jed, we were certain that the man you shot was the

one who shot our brother, weren't we? You also believed it was him, didn't you?"

"Now hold on, brother, what's goin' on here? He fit the description perfect, right down to his belly. What's the problem here? You're the one who headed us toward Purdy. How many with that description could there be in this dried-up burg?"

"I just found out he had a twin brother, and that even his momma couldn't tell 'em apart."

Jed's surprise was instantaneous. His eyes wandered crazily from Jake to the street, to some men riding by, to a dog crossing the alley behind the corral. A frown formed like black, rumbling storm clouds preparing to drench the parched desert in a downpour.

"Wh-what're you sayin'? There was two of 'em that looked exactly alike?"

"That's what I'm sayin', and that means we might have killed the wrong man. If that's so, and we did just that, we could be stretchin' a rope if anyone figures out what we were doin' here, and how we came gunnin' for him on purpose. I'm thinkin' we need to skedaddle, and pronto."

"Damn," muttered Jed. "I'll go inside and get Cutter. He needs to know what you've just told me."

Jed was inside the saloon in three long strides, saw Cutter back at the bar, and went directly to him. Cutter was between two men, laughing and tossing back whiskeys like they were water. When Jed walked up, Cutter turned to him and winked, "Well, lookee here, if it ain't my old friend Jed Bourbonette, a gunman of the first order." He had everyone's attention as he drew his revolver and waved it in the air.

His words were slurred as if he had imbibed too much cheap whiskey, and Jed could see he was going to have a tough time getting Cutter out of there before he made a big thing of everything he knew about Jed and Jake's involvement in the shooting at the saloon weeks earlier. Jed tugged at Cutter's sleeve with an urgency even a drunk should have recognized, but Cutter either didn't care or wasn't through having fun. He ignored Jed's insistent attempts to get his attention, and called to the bartender to bring him another and one for his friend.

"Ben, I, uh, need to talk to you outside. It's important."

"Now what could be so important you can't talk in front of my new pals here?" He turned, raised his drink, and continued, "Ain't that right, boys? Friends shouldn't have secrets, should they?"

Chapter Eighteen

Three or four more hours of riding at the slow pace necessitated by their wounds would bring Kelly and Two Bears within sight of Purdy. The blazing sun and Kelly's inability to stop the blood seeping from the wound in his side were taking their toll, sapping his energy. He lolled back and forth in his saddle almost as if he'd had too much whiskey. He'd slipped his rifle back into its scabbard, but kept his Colt pulled around far enough forward to get to it in a hurry if need be. Also, he had Two Bears' holster and revolver hanging on the pommel of his saddle and his rifle secured beneath his blanket roll and tied to the cantle.

Two Bears watched Kelly warily. This marshal would be a tough customer to catch off guard, even in his weakened condition. Still, he watched him carefully for any sign that he might lose consciousness and fall from his saddle. Two Bears was alert, as if he were working on a plan to take advantage if just such a turn of good fortune should befall him.

As they came down out of the foothills, a panorama of flat, dry desert lay before them. The heat rose in waves from the desert floor like a furnace stoked high enough to forge steel. What little grass there was had turned to brown from the lack of rainfall and it crunched beneath the horses' hooves. Mile after mile of scrub and cactus offered nowhere to rest in a cooling shade, nor water to drink. Kelly could feel himself nodding off into moments of restless sleep. He shook his head to maintain consciousness, but it was becoming harder and harder to remain upright in his saddle. He slumped forward, almost touching the gelding's neck. He thrust out his hand to catch the mane, but was nearly too exhausted to hold on. He was covered in perspiration.

Two Bears' wound, while painful, had stopped bleeding long ago, thanks to Kelly's quick thinking in tying it off with his neckerchief. But gratitude wasn't on the half-breed's agenda today. He had to think of himself, for, with every mile closer they came to Purdy, he could sense a noose tightening around his neck. He watched and waited for Kelly to drop from his saddle, making escape possible. It was only a matter of time before the loss of blood would take its toll.

Two Bears held no illusions that a court would

refrain from doling out the harshest punishment possible, even if he were to manage to help save the marshal, and earn a good word. The folks in town would be seeking to slip his neck into that noose for the death of old man Barker, who, it would be assumed by the inscription on the grave marker, held a deep resentment toward Two Bears over the death of his only daughter. In the case of Barker's death, in particular, it would be difficult if not impossible to stir up much sympathy from a jury. And it was anybody's guess as to how they'd feel about his gunning down Silver Pearson. The Pearsons had few friends and likely many enemies; it would still be a roll of the dice. His best option was simple, wait for Kelly to lapse into unconsciousness, and then bolt for the high country and a possible safe haven with his kin.

Kelly fought the blackness that threatened to surround him. He pushed on the pommel to try to sit straight in the saddle, but to little avail. He was weakening by the minute, and rest was his only chance of survival. But he knew he dared not stop. Such a move would emphasize his vulnerability, and there was no doubt in his mind that Two Bears would take advantage of his weakened condition to make a break for it.

Suddenly, the silence of the vast desert was broken by an echo in his head like drums in the distance. He knew it must be his own heartbeat, beating out a ghastly tempo, an insistent reminder that his body needed to replace the blood that he'd lost from the wound in his side. Then, from behind them, his attention was drawn to the source of the sound, the pounding rhythm, and the rattle of harnesses. It was the sound of a four-horse team, making its measured way across the sandy desert floor toward Purdy, pulling the Overland Express stage from Dos Cabezas, dragging a small dust cloud behind it.

As the stage neared, Kelly managed to hold up his hand to wave them down. The driver, at first not certain whether to heed the signal to stop or whip the horses into a run to avoid the chance that these two might be outlaws looking for some quick cash, had to make a decision quickly as the horses were closing in on the two. Then the flash of silver on Kelly's shirt caught the driver's attention and he shoved hard against the brake and braced himself against the kickboard as he hauled back on the reins, bringing the coach to a sliding, dusty halt.

"What can I do for you gents?" the driver said. Then he saw Kelly's bloody shirt and the pained expression on his face. He also saw the shackles that bound Two Bears.

"Damn," he muttered.

He turned to the man who was riding shotgun and ordered him to keep a sharp eye out while he jumped down. The guard didn't say a word, just secured his grip on the double-barrel Greener lying across his lap and scanned the area like a hawk looking for a rabbit. The coach was carrying only one passenger, a man in a dusty sack suit and a bowler hat. He wore a long drooping mustache and his eyes were encircled with harsh lines that bespoke a life lived hard. He looked like a near worn-out drummer, a man who had spent his life traveling from town to town peddling his wares, unable to resist drinking up the profits in the nearest saloon.

The driver helped Kelly off his gelding, and called to the guard to come down and lend a hand. The marshal struggled to stand, finding he needed to lean heavily on the two or he would surely collapse. When they got him to the stage, the driver yanked the door open.

"Mister, looks like you've got company the rest of the way into Purdy. Sorry for the inconvenience, but I reckon you'll understand," said the driver, as he helped the marshal into a seat. Kelly groaned as he slumped against the worn padding.

"Keep a gun on my prisoner, or he's likely to jump you," said Kelly. "He don't seem to have any compunction against pluggin' a man that does anything he don't like. When you get him inside, I'll shackle him to the doorpost."

The driver did as he was instructed. Afterward, he tied both horses to the baggage boot, and climbed back up into his seat.

"Hope the ride ain't too rough, folks, but we got some time to make up." With that, the driver cracked his whip and the team responded with a jerk, the horses straining at their harness as they slowly picked up their pace along the rutted and rocky road. The drummer scooted back as far into his seat as possible.

Two hours later, after several miles of rough, bumpy travel, being jostled and jerked from side to side, the stage rumbled down the only real street in Purdy. The driver called out for someone to fetch the barber for two wounded men, then he slipped from his seat to help the marshal and his prisoner out of the coach. Several men gathered around the coach to catch a glimpse of whatever had the driver hollering at the top of his voice. In minutes, the barber, Colville, came running down the middle of the street, still wiping soapy lather off his hands and onto his apron.

"What do we have here, Sam?" he said, panting. Then he saw Kelly's bloody shirt and he quickly directed some men to carry the marshal to the barbershop. A couple of the others helped Two Bears hobble along after them like a parade of stretcher-bearers leaving a battlefield. One of the men accompanying the crowd had his Remington out and ready in case Two Bears made any attempt to escape.

"Put the marshal on that table back there, fellas, and keep an eye on this one till I'm finished," he said, glancing at Two Bears with an obvious contempt. "If he don't die of lead poisonin' or leakin' too much blood first, I'll tend to him after bit."

The barber cut away the marshal's shirt from around the wound. He squinted at what he saw, then turned to dig some instruments out of a drawer.

"Gonna need some hot water to clean this mess up, gents. Someone run over to Maggie's and tell her to put a bucket on the stove. Then get it back here as fast as you can," the barber said.

"What's it look like, Mister Colville?" whispered Kelly.

"Well, sir, she cut a nice groove in your side, but it's clean and the bullet ain't in there. So, I'd say if you survive my sewin' it up, get a heapin' helpin' of Maggie's vittles, and a little sleep, I reckon you'll be as good as new in a couple days."

"What about the Indian?"

"Ain't had time to look him over, yet. He ain't bleedin' like you. Although I can't say as how there'd be much mournin' if he did kick the bucket. Folks here don't take kindly to havin' some cowpuncher come in here all high and mighty and plug our constable, worthless as he is."

"I need the man alive. He's the key to at least one murder and I aim to find out what he knows about a gang of outlaws that have been preyin' on ranchers from here to Tombstone. I'd be obliged if you'd patch him up and then see to it he has a nice, secure place to sleep in jail."

"You can rest easy, Marshal. I'll see to it he thinks he's in the Silver Palace up in Denver. Now, if you'll take a guzzle of this whiskey, it'll numb the pain some. You'll thank me for it later 'cause this needle is goin' to smart a mite."

Kelly accepted the bottle, took several swigs of the reddish-brown liquid, and then nodded to Colville to get started. The barber took the bottle from Kelly, then poured what was left over the wound. Kelly winced when the alcohol stung his flesh.

While Colville was a pretty good barber, Kelly wasn't so sure he'd ever be voted doctor of the year. But, he was the closest thing to a real sawbones Purdy had, so he would have to make do, or risk dying from a loss of blood. He gritted his teeth, and endured the pain dished out by a man he felt certain would never be asked to join the Ladies Aid Sewing Society. He passed out from the pain and loss of blood.

When he awoke several hours later, Kelly looked up to see Maggie bent over his bed. She smiled. He had been carried to his room at her boarding house by several of the locals. It felt good to have finally gotten some sleep.

"Looks like you're goin' to live. And now that you're awake, I'll fetch you some beef stew I've been lettin' simmer all day. It's got a whole heap of ripe tomatoes in it to help replace all that red stuff you been leakin' out your side." She snickered as she said it, and was still chuckling as she toddled down the hallway.

Seems like everybody in Purdy has been able to muster up a good sense of humor over my wound. Good thing I ain't goin' to die or they'd be splittin' their britches, Kelly thought.

As he lay there, staring at the ceiling, a whole new crop of questions swirled around his brain. In the morning, he'd try to get out of bed and go see Two Bears. The sooner he had his answers, the better. He wanted to move closer to solving the Albert Bourbonette murder before someone took it into his head to rid the territory of the half-breed. With the constable still unable to fulfill his duties after the shooting, the job of keeping the peace had fallen to various local citizens. And while Kelly knew these men meant to keep things calm, he wasn't so sure they'd risk getting shot if Galt and his friends decided to ride into town and drag Two Bears out of his cell. After all, he had stolen the money they figured was due them.

And to a bunch of broke cowboys, taking back what was theirs would be mighty appealing—at almost any cost.

Chapter Nineteen

Jed felt panic begin to rise up in him like a blaze in dry timber, and he broke out in a cold sweat. He was powerless to stop Cutter from mouthing off about his prowess with a gun, and how he was the one who blew some poor soul to kingdom come at Purdy's finest saloon. Then he asked if anyone had seen it. Two or three of the men shouted, "Hell, yes."

Another man spoke up, "How could you miss all the smoke and the blast from that cannon the man was a'carryin'. Coulda heard it in hell. Fact is that's probably where old Gold Pearson is right now, tryin' to figure a way to come back and haunt us all."

"And steal more of our money," shouted another.

A roar of laughter rose from the room. Somehow, either the men's general sense of humor did it, or the town was tired of thinking back on the incident, the atmosphere in the saloon went from serious to rowdy, all of it brought on by Cutter's whiskey-driven remarks. His demeanor was that of just a regular fellow with a little too much to drink in him. No one seemed moved to get revenge on Jed, or to uphold the Pearson name. In fact, it appeared the town was ambivalent to Pearson's passing.

Satisfied that they hadn't walked into a hornet's nest of townsfolk just waiting to get the opportunity to revenge Gold Pearson's death, Cutter turned to Jed and Jake and motioned them outside. They followed like sheep shaken by the appearance of a wolf at the edge of the meadow.

"Damn, Cutter, you tryin' to get us all killed, getting' drunk and talkin' like that?" said Jed.

"Found out who the fella was you killed, didn't I? Now what we got to do is nose around and dig up everything we can on him and any others he was known to ride with," said Cutter, clearly sober. "That was all part of my act. I never was drunk. Now, you two just follow my lead and we'll get this thing over and done with quick-like. And the sooner I get my other five hundred, huh, Jed?"

"Uh, yeah, sure."

Jake looked at his brother and could tell that something akin to fear was smeared all over his face. Jake had no idea where Jed came up with the five hundred he gave Cutter, but he was quite sure Jed didn't have another five hundred tucked away in that long coat of his. He didn't even know how his brother got his hands on that much cash in the first place, unless he'd lied, and actually *had* stolen it from the store in Tucson. If that was the case, the last thing Jed would want is a quick solution to finding the other three men. But Jake also knew that if Jed welched on Cutter, Jed wouldn't be the *only* target of the man's wrath. The deal had been made with both Bourbonette brothers, and that meant he was in as much danger as Jed. That being the case, he too could be walking a very thin line between life and death. He had no doubts as to Cutter's willingness to blow them both away if he thought he was being cheated out of his bounty.

"Mister Cutter, I have a suggestion, if you'd be interested in hearing it," said Jake, meekly.

"Why, sure. Nobody's ever said old Ben Cutter ain't always happy to oblige a man with a good idea. What's on your mind, son?"

"Well, I was thinking that we could cover a lot more ground if we split up, and each of us was to ask around about who this Gold Pearson ran with. It seems to me it would sit better with folks if they didn't feel like they was getting' ganged-up on by the three of us."

Cutter rubbed his chin as he thought over Jake's proposal. Preacher Ben Cutter was nobody's fool, and if an idea even smelled like it had sat in the sun too long, his reaction was reputed to be quick and fatal. He seemed a man of little patience, with a proclivity for sudden and fatal violence. But he liked the way Jake appeared to be the one standing on solid ground, trustworthy, whereas Jed appeared skittish and nervous, like he had reasons to hide the truth.

"Okay, Jake, I'll take a chance. You fellas talk things over with some of them store owners and such. They'll listen to the likes of you with your fancy duds an' all. I'll palaver with the boys in the saloon. They'll likely spill everything they know to a man like me, or be pickin' lead out of their hide for holdin' out," said Cutter. He roared at the thought, and turned on his heel, heading straight back into the saloon.

"Meet you at the hotel in a couple hours," he called back over his shoulder. "Don't be late." He was chuckling as he stomped onto the planks in front of the saloon and disappeared inside.

"What'd you do that for, Jake?"

"I need to talk to you alone before this thing goes any further. I want to know how you're going to pay Cutter if he comes up with the names of the other three, and shoots them."

"Don't worry about it. I have a plan."

"Listen, it's time you faced the hard fact that Cutter ain't a man to be trifled with. If he even thinks you're going to back out of the deal, he'll put a bullet in you so fast you won't know what hit you. And me, too. Now I want some answers, or I'm riding out of here right now. Alone."

"All right, Jake, calm down. I figure to get into a card

game and win all the money by the time we need it. I'm good with the pasteboards and I know I can come out of that saloon with the whole amount," said Jed.

Jake slumped at Jed's words, as if all the air had gone out of him. That was exactly what he figured Jed was counting on. He'd seen his brother gambling enough to know he likely wasn't as good as he thought he was. Besides, where was he going to get enough money to stake himself to a place at a table? Then, he realized there was more to Jed's plan than he was letting on. There was really only one way to get that much money, and that meant Jed meant to rob someone else. Jake shivered at the thought. They might not be as lucky this time as they had been in Tucson.

Jed had walked away from his brother and was heading for two men who were perched atop an empty hitching rail. He strode up to them as if he knew them.

"Howdy, gents. I'm new to the town. Just wondered if you'd be able to help me kinda get the lay of things," Jed said.

"Just what is it you want to know? Got lots of answers, but I'd need to know the questions first," said one of the men.

"That's right. Since I can't say we neither one of us looks too much like a fortune teller, you probably ought to come right out and say what you're about," said the other.

Jed chuckled. "Well, I was just wonderin' if there

might be an outfit lookin' to hire on a couple of men good with a six-shooter, that's about the size of it.''

One of the men squinted, trying to determine whether Jed was on the up-and-up.

"Does this look like a town tryin' to round up a range war? What would we need with a couple of gunmen? Hell, there ain't enough money hereabouts to steal, or enough cattle to rustle to justify the likes of you.''

Jed held up both hands in front of him. "Whoa, pardner, I wasn't suggestin' nothing unsavory. I didn't figure anybody would need any more owlhoots. Got enough of them already, I'm sure. I reckon we're lookin' for honest labor, but it don't hurt none if we know how to use a Colt, now does it?''

The two men looked at each other like what Jed was saying was a lot like what the liveryman has to shovel out of the stalls every night. Finally, one of them nodded, and then spoke. "Well, I reckon you could try out at the Pearson spread. I hear they've lost several men lately to unfortunate circumstances. Might be lookin' to replenish their supply." He chuckled at his own wit.

"Pearson spread, huh? How do I find out if they're hirin?''

One man hopped down from the rail and bent over to draw a map in the dirt. He explained how to locate the ranch, and told Jed the best way to avoid getting shot before he got through the gate.

"Sounds like those boys are serious about keepin' to themselves. Any reason for that?"

"Could be they don't want to have to explain how they can run a herd of no more'n fifty head of cattle, and still support near ten men. 'Course, that was before some gents gunned down Gold Pearson, and a half-breed called Two Bears shot down Silver Pearson, and then that marshal had to put an end to a couple of Pearson's bushwhackers. So, dependin' on how you look at it, whoever is left out there appears to be short-handed."

"You said both Pearson brothers are dead?"

"That's about the size of it. Either Daniel Free or that sidewinder Galt is probably in charge, now."

"How will I know either one of them?"

"Can't mistake Galt, that's for sure. He's got a scar down one cheek the size of a willow branch. As for Daniel Free, he's the only cowboy I ever did see that wears a bowler instead of something that'd keep the sun off his head."

With a look of puzzlement on his face, Jed thanked the men and walked on back to the saloon where he hoped to meet up with Jake and give him the news. He was puzzling over what he'd learned. The two men had given him more than he expected, and not all of it was good news. He saw Jake down the street, talking to a man and leaning on a stack of crates that were being unloaded from a freight wagon in front of the livery stable. A burly man was carrying the crates inside one by one, and even though they were obviously quite heavy, he handled them like they were filled with nothing more substantial than feathers. As he approached, Jake broke off the conversation and joined Jed in the middle of the street

"You learn anything useful, Jed?"

"Uh-huh. And ain't all of it good news, Jake. I remember you wrote down the descriptions of the four men that were seen at the ranch that day. You still got that with you?"

"Of course. I always take it with me, never let it out of my sight. Never know when I need to compare it to someone I suspect could be one of our killers." He took a piece of paper from his shirt pocket and unfolded it. He handed it to his brother. Jed studied it for a moment, then refolded it and handed it back to Jake. Jed's expression had turned dour; the lines around his mouth seemed to have deepened.

"We got ourselves a problem, brother. I'm beginning to wonder if your idea of riding out of here wasn't a pretty smart plan."

"A few minutes ago, you sounded like you had the whole thing figured out. Had a way to come up with the five hundred we'll owe Cutter if and when we find the men we've been lookin' for, ain't that what you said? What could have come along to change your mind?"

"I just talked to a couple of the townsfolk. Got them to give me a description of the men who are in charge out at the Pearson place, now that *both* of the Pearsons are dead."

"Both dead?"

"Yeah. They said some half-breed Indian shot the other one."

"That's good news, ain't it? Now we don't have to worry whether we got the wrong man and the right one might be plannin' a revenge," said Jake.

"That's not the problem. As I said, I got the descriptions of two that are still out there. They're dead ringers for two of the men the witnesses from Daleville said they saw at the ranch that day. What if they find out what we're here for and come gunnin' for us first?"

Chapter Twenty

Kelly was woozy the next day. Maggie had brought him stew the evening before and he'd been able to eat some, but weariness soon overtook him. He slept through the night and well into the next day. When he awoke, while anxious to get to Two Bears and begin questioning him about the murder in Daleville, he was just too weak to stand. He gave up and just lay there, staring at the ceiling, and trying to sort out what he already knew.

Maggie opened the door to his room and came in with some food. At first she thought he was still sleeping, but when he heard her footsteps, he muttered her name.

"Ahh, I almost left without feeding you, Marshal. Thought you were still asleep."

"I feel as if I could lie here for a month, Maggie. But that food does smell good, so if you'll pull that chair over here and set that plate on it, I'll try to sit up and make use of them utensils."

Maggie placed the plate as he'd asked, then stuck out a hand to help him sit up. He groaned at the attempt, but finally found himself moderately upright, though not painlessly.

"I'll be right back with some fresh Arbuckle's coffee and some more biscuits. But don't you wait for me, dig in," she said. He did just that.

When she returned minutes later, she wasn't alone. The barber, Colville, and the storekeeper, Seth Bonner, were behind her. "Got company, Marshal."

She put the coffee where Kelly could reach it, then turned to leave, but not without an admonition. "Now don't you two stay so long you wear him to a frazzle. He needs to regain his strength, and that means getting plenty of rest, not palavering with the likes of you two."

Bonner removed his hat and muttered, "Yes, ma'am." Colville grunted.

"Some fellas just rode into town, Marshal. Might be of interest to you. Thought you'd want to know soon as possible. You feelin' up to some conversation?" said Colville.

Kelly took a sip of the coffee. "Tell me what you know. I'm all right."

"Well, two fellas that look like they never did a lick of honest work come ridin' in with a big man that's a dead ringer for a gunman I once heard about in Colorado. They say he shot two men down over some woman, and he did it so damned fast they never saw him clear leather."

"You know the fella's name?"

"Nope. One of the dudes was in the saloon, drinkin' whilst the big one was blowin' off about how his drinkin' partner was the one who shot Gold Pearson."

Bonner jumped in just then. "The hotel desk clerk said the one that checked in was named Jake Bourbonette, and he took a room for three. That name mean anything to you, Marshal?"

"Hmm. Yep, that name might save me a long ride, especially if there's two of 'em here."

"Well, there was two of 'em in the saloon and they looked like they could be kin. I seen 'em go outside with the big fella, the one that looks like a shootist," said Colville.

"Why don't you go over to the jail, Mister Colville, and see if you can find any dodgers on the one you say you heard about in Colorado. See if there's anybody lookin' for him," said Kelly.

"Yessir, I'll do just that. Want I should do anything else?"

"Not just yet. Mister Bonner, would you consider keepin' a watch over what them three appear to be up to? Staying a safe distance from them, of course."

"Be happy to oblige, Marshal."

"Get back here lickety-split if you see trouble startin' to brew, either of you."

"Oh, Mister Colville, how is Two Bears?"

"He'll live long enough to hang, I reckon. You getting the bleedin' stopped saved him from the same thing that happened to you. Too bad you only carry one kerchief," Colville said with a smirk.

"Is he safely in jail?"

"He ain't goin' nowhere. I can promise that. We'll keep him fed and fattened up for the judge."

Colville and Bonner both left just as Maggie returned with some more coffee.

"They sure seemed in a hurry to wash their hands of this place, like their britches was full of scorpions."

"I sent Colville and Bonner out to be my eyes and ears while these stitches heal a bit more. By the way, this food sure does hit the spot, Maggie. Thanks for everything."

"Think nothing of it, Marshal. It's comfortin' to know I got a real man under my roof for a change. Most of what passes through here ain't fit to clean the stables. Some of them that stay over every now and again from the Pearson spread are ornery, good-for-nothing rattlers."

"Isn't Daniel Free one of Pearson's men? I believe I saw him at your table the day I came."

"That was him, all right. He's the closest one to a decent soul of 'em all, but he ain't no angel by any stretch, no sir. Like as not he'd put a bullet in you if he figured you were coming between him and whatever he wants at the time, which is mostly money."

"Uh-huh. I'm pretty sure it was either him or the one called Galt that shot me and Two Bears."

"Why would he do that? You don't have anything he'd want, do you?"

"Maybe I do, Maggie. Maybe I do."

"And what would that be?"

"I'll let you know just as soon as I find out what the Bourbonette brothers are doing here."

"I understand you have to keep all this nasty business pretty secret. But if you need a body to confide in, you just give me a holler." Maggie left the room with a wink and a spring in her step.

Kelly finished eating and collapsed back onto the bed. He lay there watching a fly crawling across the ceiling, mulling over what his next move might be. The Bourbonettes had come here once before, when Jed shot Gold Pearson. Why were they back? Were they actually on a mission of revenge, and how did they put the Pearsons together with their brother's killing? He went to sleep before any answers came to him.

It was late that day when Kelly awoke. His body seemed to have benefited from some food and plenty of rest. Although somewhat painful from Colville's stitches tugging at his skin, he was able to sit up and even get out of bed without much trouble. *That's good*, he thought, *now maybe I can get back to finding who shot us*. He slipped into his shirt, which Maggie had kindly washed and sewn up the hole where the bullet had ripped through. He put on his boots, gun belt, and hat, and went to the dining room to see if he could find some coffee. Maggie was cleaning the table when he entered the room.

"Marshal, I was just gonna come see if you were awake and would like some soup. I made up a batch of vegetable soup that'll put hair on your chest," she giggled.

"I don't need anything to eat right now, Maggie, but thanks anyway. I wouldn't mind a cup of coffee if you have any left, though."

"You just sit yourself down and I'll bring the pot." She left the room briefly to clank around in the large kitchen, returning with a porcelain cup and a steaming pot.

As he sat there, sipping coffee so hot it would scald the hide off a buffalo, he tried to consider his options. The more he thought about it, the more certain he was that Two Bears was the key to whatever might happen next. And although he had no idea what might be going through the mind of some foolhardy, gun-toting cowboy with a grudge, he figured he'd better go talk to the half-breed before anything happened to him. He couldn't afford to lose a prisoner to the likes of Galt, or one of his followers. And, as well as keeping a tight lookout for any of Pearson's men, he also had to figure out why the Bourbonettes were in town accompanied by a gunslinger. He could only speculate as to what their intentions might be.

Kelly left Maggie's carrying his Winchester carbine. He carried the rifle with him almost everywhere he went, always with the chamber containing a round ready to fire. He went straight to the jail. When he got there, he found the constable propped up on a cot in the corner of the room. Colville was seated at the desk with his head lying on a stack of papers sound asleep. When Kelly clomped into the room, Colville awoke with a start. He sat up, rubbed his eyes, and put his spectacles back on.

"Ah, Marshal, good to see you up and around. I been goin' through these posters and haven't seen hide nor hair of the gent in question."

"How is the prisoner?" Kelly asked.

"He's gettin' along—" Colville began.

"The dirty little rat will live at least long enough for me to heal up and hang him from the nearest rafter myself," grumbled the constable.

"Well, I need to talk to him before you throw him to the wolves," said Kelly.

"Suit yourself, Marshal. I don't think I'll be up to objectin' to much of anything until this leg heals."

Kelly went into the back room where the single cell stood. It wasn't one of the more traditional steel bar cells, but rather a wooden room, made from heavy timbers and beams brought down from Colorado. The door was at least as strong as any steel bars, and made escape harder because the only access was a small window where food was slipped to the prisoner. Kelly took the keys and unlocked the padlock that secured a piece of bar steel, allowing the door to swing open.

"Come on out of there, Two Bears. It's time to have a conversation."

The Indian had been asleep on the bunk when the marshal jarred him awake by rattling the keys and sliding the bar open. He sat up cautiously, almost as if he half-expected to be yanked out and strung up before he had his trial. He hobbled to the door, looked around to make sure the marshal was the only one there, and left the cell.

"Looks like they patched you up proper, Marshal. Glad to see you're up and around, yessir, mighty glad. You saved my neck once, I hope you're still in a mood to see I don't meet with no foul play before a judge sees to it I'm a free man."

"What makes you think you'll be freed, Two Bears?"

"I know things, things I'm plannin' on usin' to bargain my way out of here. Bet you'd like to know what they are, too."

"Strange as it may seem, that's the very thing I've come to discuss with you."

Kelly pulled a pair of arm shackles from a peg on the wall, and clamped them on Two Bears as the constable and Colville looked on with expressions of puzzlement. The marshal took his prisoner by the arm and led him to the door.

"Uh, where is it you're plannin' on takin' the skunk, Marshal? I ain't keen on losing the man that shot me, and clubbed you, too, if you'll think back on it."

"Don't worry, he's not goin' far. We need to have a

little sit-down and it needs to be private. I'll have him back before long," Kelly said with a tip of his Stetson. He pushed Two Bears through the door and out onto the boardwalk with the barrel of his rifle.

"We're goin' over to the boardin' house, Two Bears. We'll have lots of privacy there, and you can tell me everything you know without fear of being overheard. Then, if I like what you tell me, I'll bring you back here, instead of hanging you from the balcony of the hotel myself. You do understand what I'm sayin', don't you?"

Two Bears nodded nervously.

Chapter Twenty-one

Cutter strode up to the brothers and motioned for them to join him in the saloon. They followed him inside and took a table near a front window. Jed and Jake both sat forward, elbows on the table as if awaiting some momentous news. Cutter had news for them all right, but he wasn't certain it would be all that welcome. He'd long ago learned that staying in the saloon and keeping your eyes and ears open was the best place to learn about all the comings and goings of any community. Purdy was no different.

"Well, boys, I been talkin' to some of the locals and they can get pretty talkative after a little liquor."

"I learned some mighty interestin' things myself, Mister Cutter. While you was in here soppin' up the local gossip, I found out that two of the men out at the

Pearson ranch fit the description of the men who were seen at our ranch to a 'T'," said Jed.

"That right?"

"Yessir, that's right."

"And what do you figure to do about it?"

"Uh, I guess I figured you'd, er, want to go out there and, uh, maybe face 'em down," stammered Jed.

"Don't know if you happened to notice a couple of men that came into town on the stage all bloodied up. One of them was a U.S. Marshal. The other was a no-account half-breed named Two Bears. He's over in the jail, locked up good an' tight."

"Two Bears? Why, I was told that was the name of the fella that shot down the other Pearson brother, Silver I think his name was."

Throughout the conversation Jake was becoming increasingly nervous. He could see Jed pushing things right up to a showdown, a showdown he had no money to pay for, and only a scant chance of actually winning enough at the poker tables to make it up. The reckless way his brother was behaving was giving him chills and a growing desire to get shuck of this dirty little town as fast as he could.

"You already got a plan for how you expect me to take on the whole damn bunch? I'm good, but I didn't figure on havin' to face down more'n one at a time." Cutter growled.

"No. That's your business. You figure it however you've a mind to," said Jed. "But we can't let these weasels slip out of our hands. Now that we got a real good notion who we're after, I say we look to forcin' a showdown."

"We?" said Cutter, his eyebrows raised questioningly.

"You know what I mean. We hired you 'cause you're right good with that six-shooter. When all our cards are on the table, I'm lookin' to you to handle the situation, Cutter, like I *know* you will," said Jed.

He began tapping on the table with his fingernails, beating out a rhythm that said he was through talking about a subject. It was a signal to those who knew him that he was growing impatient. This was a habit Jake had seen as his brother was growing up. Whenever he was up against a situation that required him to exercise tolerance, to adjust to someone else's timetable, he'd tense up and begin tapping his foot or rocking back and forth. The night they walked into the Sure Shot Saloon, preparing to face Gold Pearson, Jed had begun tapping his whiskey glass on the bar.

If *he* could see Jed's impatience with the way things were going, then Cutter surely could, too. That knowledge could work in Cutter's favor. How, he couldn't be certain, but he knew it was likely to be in some way that might put Jed in an untenable situation. Whenever Jed was shoved into a corner, he acted without any forethought to the consequences. And people in too much of a hurry risk getting hurt.

"Don't you worry about how I handle things. But don't get in my way or you may find yourself in the middle of a bloody mess. Now, you wouldn't want that, would you, little friend?" Cutter's eyes narrowed, and his hand went for the butt of his revolver.

"Uh, n-no, surely not," stammered Jed, suddenly aware of his own propensity for getting the cart before the horse, and speaking before he thought. "I-I'm sorry if I gave the wrong impression. Y-you're the boss."

Cutter just grinned and looked away. He now had himself in exactly the position he sought, the high ground. He had Jed right where he wanted him—scared and subservient.

Cutter pushed his chair back and got up. He downed the last of his whiskey, then marched to the door and went outside. Jed and Jake followed.

"Where are you headed?" asked Jake.

"I'm goin' down to the jail and have me a talk with that constable. You two wait here. I'll be back in a bit."

Jake went back inside, while Jed stood there not quite sure which way to turn. Finally, he followed Jake back to the table they'd just left. Jake sat with a worried look, while Jed looked like a scared rabbit, certain that a hungry coyote was just inches away.

"What's got you so frazzled, Brother? Cutter doesn't make you nervous, does he? After all, it was your idea to hire a gunman to solve our problem. You do remember that, don't you?"

Jed held up his hand and motioned for the bartender to bring some whiskey. He sat with both hands on the table, drawing circles in the spills. He nodded to Jake.

"Yeah, I reckon Cutter does make me a mite jumpy. And, yeah I know he was my idea. Maybe I'm just havin' second thoughts about that."

"Well, it's too late to worry about it now. We got to figure a way out of here when he gets those other men and finds out we got no way to pay him the rest of his fee. So, how about you get to thinkin' on that, since you seem to be the one with all the bright ideas." Jake crossed his arms and scooted down in his chair. He'd thrown down the gauntlet and would now wait for Jed to pick it up. He was aware of just how unlikely that was, so he began quietly mulling over the situation in his own mind, hoping against hope that some solution would come to him like a bolt of lightning. He sighed to himself as he realized just how few serious problems he'd had to face in his life. Storekeeping hadn't proven to be a job fraught with life or death circumstances, at least not thus far. Although, from the start, it had been a losing proposition.

Jed poured a shot of whiskey and downed it like it was water, not the bitter, watered-down product of a saloon owner's greed. He knew liquor was never a path to victory over adversity, but there were times when he wished it was. This was one of those times.

Cutter stomped through the door to the jail. He stopped, looked around, then he spotted the constable sound asleep on a cot in the corner, near a pot-bellied stove, a small flame burning in its belly, just enough to keep the coffee pot atop the burner warm. Constable Jackson lifted his head at the sound of Cutter's entrance. He tried to sit up, but found he could only rise up on one elbow. That would have to do as he eyed the stranger in front of him.

"What can I do for you, stranger?" he said with a sleepy yawn.

"I've come to see your prisoner, the Indian fella," said Cutter.

"And just who would be askin' for this visit, and what would be your business with him?"

"Name's Cutter. Some folks call me Preacher Ben, but I never put much faith in monikers others stick on a man. And as to my reason for bein' here, well I just want to ask the man a few questions, that's all."

Jackson was more than familiar with the name and it struck fear in him. He'd heard the stories about the man with no conscience who would cut a man down for no more reason than having a bad feeling about him, or not caring for the way he was dressed. Now here was this killer right in front of him, and him not able to fully sit up by himself, let alone put up some sort of defense if it became necessary. In fact the nearest gun was a rifle in the rack behind his desk all the way across the room. He knew darn well this man wasn't here just to ask a few questions. He had something far more serious on his mind, but what?

"Well, Mister Cutter, I hope you'll forgive me if I don't rise and shake the hand of a man well-known in these parts, but I'm afraid I've fallen victim to a bullet in the thigh, put there, I might add, by the very man you've made inquiry of."

"Ain't necessary for any formal howdy, Constable, make yourself comfortable right where you are. I'm just askin' to take up a few minutes of the man's time in hopes he can steer me in the right direction concerning a problem I have," said Cutter.

"And what would that problem be?"

"I reckon I can confide in an honest lawman to keep any information I might impart as confidential, ain't that right?"

"That you surely can, sir, that you can."

"Well, you see, I've been hired by a couple of gents to look into the unfortunate death of their brother. And I've been led to believe this Two Bears fella can put me on the trail of the men who did this dastardly thing to an unarmed man."

"Hmmm, yes I see why you'd like to discuss the matter with the breed. But I have to be very careful who I let into the back, since I can't walk you back there myself. Now who was it you say hired you?"

"I didn't say, but it was Jake and Jed Bourbonette."

"Now that's mighty interestin'. The name of the fella that rode in here and shot Gold Pearson was named Bourbonette, if I ain't mistaken. That wouldn't be the same man that hired you, would it?"

"I don't know the particulars about that shooting, but I assume we are talking about the same individual, yes."

"That would tend to put a different light on the situation." Jackson rubbed his stubbly chin as he struggled to come up with a way to send this man off without an unseemly incident, which would surely ensue if he couldn't shake him off Two Bears' trail. He didn't really care for the half-breed, but he didn't want to see him gunned down, either, which was exactly what he saw as Cutter's real intent.

"What kind of questions were you lookin' to ask the breed?"

Cutter's mannerisms showed he was weary of the conversation with the crippled old lawman, a conversation that was obviously meant to send him down some rabbit hole.

His patience at an end, he gritted his teeth as he blurted out, "Listen, old man, I came here politely asking to see your prisoner. That's all. Now do I get to see him or not?"

Jackson winced at the implication in Cutter's voice. He hated to do it, but he saw no other course to take. He had to tell the truth.

"I'm sorry, Mister Cutter, but Two Bears isn't in my jail. He was escorted out of here several hours ago, and he ain't been brought back."

"Taken away? Who could do that?"

"Another lawman, that's who. In this case, it was U.S. Marshal Piedmont Kelly. And I didn't push too hard as to when he meant to return him."

Chapter Twenty-two

Maggie met Kelly and Two Bears at the door.

"What've you a mind to do bringin' that two-bit scoundrel into a decent, God-fearin' house, Marshal? I got no truck with the likes of him," Maggie said with a frown that could turn a sunny day cloudy.

"Don't worry, Maggie, I don't figure he'll be here long. Just long enough for him to tell me what he knows about that Pearson operation without every ear in town being in on the hearin'. We won't put you out none, nor bring you any trouble. You got my word on it."

Two Bears scrambled to remove his weather-beaten old slouch hat, drawing it down in front of him to cover the fact that he was wearing shackles.

"Well, I'll take you at your word. But mind you, if he causes any stir, or scuffs up a stick of furniture, you can count on this old woman makin' herself mighty hard to handle with a broomstick in her hands."

A smile crept across Kelly's lips as he responded, "I'll keep that in mind, ma'am, I surely will." He pushed Two Bears in front of him, herding him into the sitting room at the front of the house, just off the porch.

"Sit over there," he said. The Indian nodded grudgingly. He looked at his clothing, briefly comparing its sad state of affairs to the nice chair with a crocheted coverlet. He hesitated, then sat.

"What is it you want to know, Marshal?"

"There are some men in town who lost a brother a year ago. The four men who likely killed him were seen leaving his ranch outside of Daleville."

"What's that got to do with me?"

"I got a hunch you were one of the four men, and if not, you probably know who they were."

"Why would you think that?"

"One of the men who shot Gold Pearson is the brother of the man who was killed. I think he hunted Gold down and shot him in revenge for his brother Albert's murder. That man and his brother are back in Purdy, probably lookin' for the other three men. I'm just tryin' to clear this thing up without anyone getting' killed. Those boys, and a killer they're ridin' with, won't be so patient."

"Whatever gave them the idea that Gold Pearson had anything to do with killin' this man?"

"The constable found the man's gold watch on

Gold's body. There was an inscription on the back with Albert's name. If he didn't have anything to do with it, how'd he get that watch?"

Two Bears suddenly became very nervous. He fidgeted in his chair, wrinkling his face like a man trying to twist his way out of a noose. His eyes darted about, searching for where his next words might come from.

"What's in it for me if I tell you what you want to know?"

"It all depends on what you tell me. I may be able to get the constable to go easy on you for shootin' him, and I'm willin' to drop any charges over you tryin' to crack my skull. The Barker and Pearson shootings, well, we'll just have to see. I do know this, I'm your only chance at getting' out of here alive."

"Wh-what do you mean?"

"I figure Pearson's man, Galt, and his friend, Free, are lookin' to even the score for their boss, and get back that money you took from his house. Then there are the Bourbonette brothers and their hired gunman who are trying to find anyone connected to their brother's murder. And, of course, the town ain't too happy about you pluggin' their constable, not to mention Barker's unhappy end. Reckon there's a heap of trouble brewin' for you all around."

Seeing no way out of his entanglement, Two Bears sighed.

"Okay, I'll tell you what I can, which, mind you,

ain't much. It may not be near what you're expectin' to hear, either. But here goes."

Kelly sat silently as the breed took a deep breath and began his long-winded tale.

"I was runnin' from the law over near Appaloosa when I ran into the Pearsons. They were lookin' to round up a few men handy with a gun, and I signed on. When I got to the Pearson ranch, it was clear there weren't enough work around that run-down place to keep a body in beer or bullets. When I asked what it was they did to keep the ranch alive, they told me to be patient, they'd tell me when the time was right. Well, sir, the time got right within a week," he said, then paused.

"Go on."

"Say you don't suppose the lady could round up something to parch a man's thirst, do you? I'm drier'n a two-foot well."

"I'll see what I can do." Kelly hollered for Maggie. She came running into the room as if she was expecting to see it in shambles.

"What is it? Is everything all right?"

"Yes, Maggie, everything is fine. But I wonder if you could find it in your heart to round up a couple of cups of that wonderful coffee you brew. I think it might help my, uh, interview with this man go better."

Relieved at finding things in the same condition as when she left, Maggie said she'd be happy to oblige, and she rushed out of the room in such a hurry she nearly knocked over a small table just outside the double-doors.

"Uh, coffee wasn't exactly what I had in mind, Marshal. Ain't there even a thimbleful of something a bit more bitey around this joint?"

"I'm afraid not. Besides, considerin' the effect liquor appears to have on you, I might have to shoot you, myself."

Maggie returned with two cups and a pot of steaming Arbuckles on a tray. She placed the tray on a table next to the couch, then poured coffee into each cup. As she reached forward with a cup for Two Bears, she stiffened at the sight of his shackles, then, with a pained smile, thrust it in front of him.

"Uh, I'm obliged, ma'am," said Two Bears. Maggie slipped from the room quickly.

"All right, now you've got something to wet your whistle, get on with your story," said Kelly.

"A bite of something to eat would help, too, you know. I ain't had nothin' to eat since you brung me in."

Kelly eased his Colt from its holster, half-cocked it, and rolled the cylinder through a couple of times. He sat back, gently placing the gun on the table next to him.

Two Bears took another sip of coffee before speaking. "I, uh, reckon I can wait a while longer for them vittles. Uh, now where were we?"

"You were about to tell me what your job would be for the Pearsons."

"Yeah, well you see, it was this way. By the way, what I'm about to tell you can't get me in more trouble, can it?"

"Get on with it and no more stallin'."

"Sure. Sure. Well, Gold told me we was goin' on a little trip. When I asked where, all he said was it'd be to pick up our salaries. I didn't understand until we headed for the river valley. Soon as we started into that part that widens out some between the mountains, where all them little one-horse ranches are, he stopped us and gave us the plan."

"Go on."

"What he meant to do was to pick out the small ranches, the ones that would likely not have anybody hangin' around but a cook and maybe somebody fixing harness. He said everybody else would be out tendin' to their measly herds. He picked a time when the cows would be calvin' so's they'd be sure to be away. We was to ride in quick-like, and hit the place like ol' Quantrill took that town in Kansas," said Two Bears, occasionally stopping to sip his coffee.

"Well, it worked like he said it would. We never got much, but it was enough to keep us goin'. Most of them small ranchers didn't put a lot of trust in banks. Gold knew that, and figured they'd keep whatever cash they had real handy like. And just to make sure none of us got to spoutin' off in town 'bout where we got the money, he kept it all in that tin box. He bought all the food, supplies, clothing, most anything we needed."

"But what was the plan if anyone resisted?"

"Some did, of course, but that was why the plan was so good. We'd size up the number of hands by watchin' from a distance for a few hours. That way we knew who'd be there when we rode in. Then a couple of us would stick a gun in the ribs of any who felt they was being wronged, and after the Pearsons got everything of value, we'd ride out pretty as you please. Musta hit ten, twelve places in one month."

"And what happened to those that did put up some objection?"

"Nothin'. We'd just tie 'em up and ride out."

"Then what happened to the man who was shot?"

"There wasn't no man got shot. 'Least ways, not while I was ridin' with 'em. Honest. We never killed nobody."

Kelly had no idea whether the Indian was telling the truth or not. The man certainly hadn't built up a reputation for honesty or good judgment. But if he was playing it straight, then someone else had to have been the killer. There were still answers he needed from this man.

"How long did you ride with that outfit?"

"Ever since I signed on goin' on a year and a half, I reckon."

"Did you go on every raid?"

"Far as I know, yeah. There were five of us: Gold, Silver, Galt, Daniel Free, and myself. Only four went into the ranches, the other stood watch where he could see anybody a'comin' and warn the others."

"How many ranches did you hit altogether?"

"Been doin' it for awhile, so I reckon we musta robbed about fifty, sixty of 'em."

"How much do you figure you got from each ranch?"

"Lots of 'em were pretty puny. Maybe fifty, seventy-five dollars at the most. But some, like one over near Cochise, got us about five hundred. Pretty good haul for a small ranch operation," Two Bears said, almost with pride. He certainly was showing no remorse for his part in the activities of the Pearson gang. "We got enough to keep us goin'."

"I have the box you took from the ranch. I haven't opened it yet. How much do you figure I'll find in there when I do?"

"Got no idea. But it ought to be sizable," grinned Two Bears.

Kelly was filled with mixed emotions about the man sitting across from him. There was a strange kind of likeability to his manner, but one couldn't help but wonder how he'd grown into manhood, seemingly without one hint of an understanding of basic morality.

Since Two Bears was the only connection he had that might lead him to who killed Albert Bourbonette, he had little choice but to try his best to protect him, at least until he had elicited all the information he could about the Pearsons' activities.

"What do you know about the watch that was found on Gold Pearson when he was shot?" said Kelly.

"Not much. Just that he carried it around all the time.

Called it his lucky piece. Some gambler was down to his last penny and the pot was big. He let the gambler toss the watch on the pile in place of cash. Reckon that gambler figured he had the winning hand. But he didn't. Gold won the hand and took it all. Ever since then, he'd clung to that gold watch like it was a magic charm or something," said Two Bears.

Chapter Twenty-three

Cutter stormed out of Constable Jackson's office. He'd put up with the old man's questions for long enough, all of which had led to nothing more than a delaying tactic. He was angry, and Preacher Ben Cutter wasn't a pleasant man to be around when he was calm, but when angered, the reputation that followed him around like a hungry wolf suggested he could become a most fearsome adversary when provoked. He returned to the saloon determined to elicit more information about the men he was supposed to be on the trail of, and get some answers about things that had been bothering him from the beginning. Things like, "Why did you wait a year before it came to you to chase these varmints down?"

That question was the first thing out of his mouth when he joined the brothers back at the saloon.

"What difference does it make?" said Jake. "All that matters is that it came to me, that's all."

"Yeah, and I didn't even know about it until I came back to Daleville recently," said Jed. "Why is it important?"

"Seems important to me. If my kin was shot down and I didn't do anything about it, I'd have trouble closin' my eyes at night. I 'spect I'd be riddled with guilt for bein' a coward."

Jed jumped to his feet at the thinly veiled accusation. "Listen, Cutter, whatever it is or isn't that you would have done, ain't no concern of mine, nor Jake's. It happened, that's all. Now let it be, or else."

Cutter made no move as he waited for Jed to either cool down or go for his gun. By remaining calm, hardly anyone had noticed he'd returned to the saloon and taken up residence at the table near the window. Now, however, all eyes were on the angry young man standing making threatening gestures and shouting at the known gunman. Suddenly Jed realized he was the center of attention. His faced flushed as he eased back down into his chair, as the room slowly returned to its normal buzz of conversation, satisfied that the excitement had died of its own accord.

"Hope you feel better now, sonny. But you still ain't answered my question," said Cutter, as calmly as if he'd just awoken from a nap. "And just what did you mean by, 'or else?'"

Jed drew his hands up in front of him and hung his head.

"Well, Mister Cutter, as for me, I can tell you that I didn't have any idea how to go about findin' those men. Reckon I didn't have the gumption, neither. At the funeral, I was so ashamed that I hadn't ridden out to see Albert more often I think I wept openly. I had largely ignored him after he bought out my share and I opened my business in town. The sheriff swore he'd find whoever did it, and I let him handle it. Even though I think I felt deep down that he wouldn't ever find them. And he didn't," said Jake.

"And you, Jed, what did you do after you left the ranch?"

"I'm a gambler, natural born. I followed that trail all the way down to New Orleans, up and down the Mississippi, and back, 'cross Texas and New Mexico, from Fort Worth to Albuquerque and Santa Fe. Never was interested in runnin' no stinkin' ranch," said Jed. "So I ran away from it. Reckon, in a way, I'm still runnin'."

Jed had calmed down and returned to his seat, still fuming inside over Cutter's constant digging into what Jed felt was none of Cutter's business. Jed scooted down in his chair as if to let others know there was no cause for alarm and perhaps make himself a little less noticeable in doing so. He hadn't liked Cutter from the beginning, but had seen in the gunman a way to solve a problem, about which he was now having second thoughts.

It was late afternoon when Galt and Daniel Free rode into Purdy. A hot wind was blowing, indicating the onset of a dry storm. A scrawny mutt crossed the street in front of them, hesitating every few feet to look behind for signs of a pursuer, then it scurried under the boardwalk that ran in front of the saloon. The two stopped, dismounted, and draped their horses' reins over the rail. Galt scanned the street for signs of a familiar face, and seeing none, turned to Free, who was also nervously looking around.

"Two Bears and the marshal must be here. Let's have ourselves a drink before we go bargin' in on ol' Constable Jackson," said Galt. "Got to make sure no one's lookin' for us."

"Okay. But only one. We may have to shoot our way out of this town if he don't see things our way."

They went straight to the bar upon entering the saloon. Several cowboys were standing with glasses of beer in their hands, and a couple of tables had card games in progress. Smoke filled the room. The good-natured laughter they'd heard as they entered died down almost instantly as some of the men recognized Galt and Free. Neither of the men were popular in Purdy, especially since they had always been suspect as to their method of obtaining money. Everyone had heard stories of the many robberies of small ranches all up and down the San Pedro for several years. No one had been caught, and no real evidence pointed to the Pearson bunch, but suspicions ran high that they had somehow been involved.

"A couple of beers, bartender," Galt said as he pushed between two men at the bar. Free followed. Both took out some coins and dropped them on the polished wood surface as the bartender drew the foaming brew into a glass.

When they were served, the two sought a table as far from the rest of the patrons as possible. They sat with their backs to the wall, watching every movement like they were afraid of being gunned down, though for no understandable reason. Both seemed jumpy, and overly cautious. Those may have been the very attributes that had caused so many to suspect the Pearson boys, each of whom acted the same skittish way whenever they were in town. Galt sipped his beer; Free downed his in two long gulps. He wiped his mouth with the back of his hand, then leaned forward.

"I don't like this, Galt. We should have gone directly to the jail, demanded that the constable turn over Two Bears, if he has him, and got ourselves out of town, pronto. I feel like every eye in this dump is borin' a hole in my skull, each one thinkin' he'd like to put a bullet in both of us."

Galt didn't say a word; he just kept staring straight ahead at the swinging doors to the saloon. Every once in a while another cowboy or miner would tromp in, bringing with him the dust and smell of sweaty horses.

"Galt, are you listenin'?"

"I hear you, Free. Leave me alone, I'm thinkin'."

"Thinkin' about what? There ain't nothin' to think about. We got to get back what rightly belongs to us, namely that tin of money Two Bears stole. And we need to be gettin' at it, now."

"Ain't there somethin' you're forgettin', Daniel?"

"Like what?"

"Like one pesky United States Marshal. You don't figure he's goin' to just sit back, lollygaggin' around while we grab that loot from all them robberies, and in the process pay that Indian back for what he did to Silver, do you?"

"Well, no, I don't 'spect he will. But he's bound to have a healthy respect for a .44. There's two of us to one of him, so what's there to worry about?"

"You didn't stand there in front of him with them gray eyes staring a hole in *your* soul. You saw it yourself; he ain't just some ordinary man. He's got ice in his veins instead of blood. Cold like a north wind in January. I want to know where he is and what he's up to before I go stickin' my nose in that jail."

Free leaned back and thought for a moment about what Galt had said. He ran his tongue back and forth across his teeth, frowning. He was uncomfortable sitting, waiting for Galt to make a move. He was about to go outside where he didn't feel corralled.

He started to push out of his chair, when, without warning, Galt sprang up, motioned for Free to follow, and the two shoved through the double doors and out into the street. When they got outside, Galt turned to Free and said, "Did you take notice of them three at the far table? The big man looked to be good with a piece. I've seen him somewhere before. And the other two kept starin' at us."

"So what?"

"Remember what some of the boys said when Gold got himself gunned down? They said there were two brothers, dark hair, thin-faced. If that's them, why do you figure they were lookin' at us so hard? We never did nothin' to them."

Free rubbed his chin. "That's a good question. Makes it even more important that we get what we're after and vamoose. The longer we stay here, the greater the danger. All those ranches we been hitting, there's bound to be someone here who remembers one of us. In our business a man's bound to make enemies. Let's get outta here and go have us a talk with that constable."

When they got to the jail, Galt stopped to look around, to make certain they hadn't been followed, and that the marshal wasn't anywhere to be seen. But the street was empty, except for a slow moving freight wagon driven by a Mexican in a wide-brimmed sombrero.

Galt entered the door to the jail first. He stopped at the sight of the constable lying on the small bed, snoring soundly. Their entrance had not awakened Jackson.

Galt tiptoed over to the door to the back and peeped through the small window. The single jail cell was empty. He turned and gave the stove a kick, knocking over the poker. It crashed to the floor with the expected result. Jackson shot up to a half-sitting position and stared angrily at Galt.

"What the hell are you doin' here, Galt? And why all the confounded racket?"

"We're lookin' for Two Bears. Where the hell is he?"

"And just what business it of yours where that no-good might be, you trouble-makin' varmint?"

"Need to talk to him about a little matter that needs settlin'."

"Well, you're a little late. A U.S. Marshal done took him outta here for parts unknown. Ain't got any idea where they are, nor do I care. Now get your worthless hide out of my office and let me get back to my sleep."

Galt's impatience had reached its limits. He reached out and grabbed the corpulent constable by his lapels and pulled hard.

"Listen here, you lousy excuse for a lawman, I said I'm lookin' for Two Bears to settle a score and I don't aim to ride out without seein' it through," growled Galt. Free stood near the door, checking constantly to make sure they wouldn't be disturbed before Galt's temper had run its course.

"He ain't here, and I don't know where he is. Now git!" yelled Jackson.

Daniel reached out and tugged on Galt's shirtsleeve as he saw the man's fingers twitch and start for his gun.

"It ain't worth it, Galt. Let's skedaddle and find him ourselves. How far can they have gotten? I'm certain one of us put a slug into him. He probably needed some doctorin' and I'll bet Colville will know where they got to. C'mon."

Galt shoved the constable back onto his bed and stormed out the door. Free gave a sigh of relief and followed closely behind.

Chapter Twenty-four

Kelly sat puzzled by Two Bears' explanation of how Gold Pearson came to be in possession of Albert Bourbonette's gold watch. There was something about the whole story that didn't make sense. Now, with the added knowledge that there were at least two men from the Pearson ranch seeking vengeance on Two Bears for one reason or another, Kelly was faced with a hard decision—how to keep his prisoner alive long enough to sort out exactly who did kill the man in Daleville. As he rubbed his chin with a pensive frown, Maggie entered the room.

"Would you like a little more coffee before I throw the rest out? It's done set around too long to keep its flavor," she said.

"No, thank you, ma'am." Then a thought occurred to

him. Perhaps keeping Two Bears out of the line of fire wouldn't be as hard as he thought.

Just then, Colville knocked at the front door and entered the parlor before Maggie could say anything. "Sorry to bust in like this, Maggie, but I got to talk to the marshal."

"That's all right. You go right on in."

Colville removed his hat and slipped through the heavy drapes that hung at the parlor's wide doorway.

"Marshal, I got some news. The big fellow that came to town with them two brothers went down to the jail, and when he come out, he wasn't lookin' real happy. Then just a few minutes ago, I seen Galt and Daniel Free come ridin' in. They are over at the saloon, or at least they was when I slipped out to come tell you. I'd swear they're lookin' for trouble too."

Kelly was silent as he pondered Colville's words. He had known from the time he and Two Bears rode into town, all shot up, that there would come a time when he'd have to deal with those whose intentions went counter to the law he was sworn to uphold. And now it seemed the time had come to deal with men who had murder on their minds. Maybe more of them than he'd hoped to deal with.

"Maggie, I wonder if you'd consider doin' me a favor. A mighty big one."

"Why, sure, if I can, Marshal. I'd be proud to help the law in any way I'm able."

"The storeroom in the back, it ain't got any windows

in it as I recall. And the door is pretty stout, with a lock on it, right?"

"Yep. Had it built that way so no one could sneak in and steal food when I was asleep. And that lock ain't just no ordinary one, neither; it's a genuine Yale & Towne. Best you can buy. Seth Bonner sent all the way to St. Louis to get it for me. It'll hold 'bout anything."

"How about a prisoner? This here one, for instance," Kelly said, hooking a thumb in Two Bears' direction.

The look that came over Maggie's face could have boiled water. Kelly could see the clouds gathering in her eyes and the questions forming on her lips, along with her unsaid reluctance to be a part of whatever scheme the marshal had in mind. He wasn't all that confident about it himself, but his options seemed to be narrowing by the minute.

"I, uh, don't know about that, Marshal. What's wrong with the jail we got?"

"Some men have come to town who want to see Two Bears dead. The jail's the first place they'll look. When they find he's gone, I'm hopin' they'll either go away or seek me out. Then I can try to solve this standoff directly, without them trying to make a run on the jail. A jail with a wounded constable who can hardly stand, let alone defend himself. I only need to keep Two Bears out of the line of fire for a few hours. Just a safe place to stash him so he don't get shot before I can haul him before a judge."

Maggie hung her head and thought about what the

marshal was proposing. She frowned at what seemed to be about to happen in her town, but her expression showed she was powerless to change the direction events seemed to be taking. Finally, she sighed and said, "All right, Marshal, I reckon if it's the only way to keep a man from gettin' shot before he gets a fair trial, I can't stand in the way of justice. Just you be sure my place don't end up a shootin' gallery."

"You got my word on it, Maggie."

"I'll hold you to it, too," she said, with a mischievous grin.

Kelly pulled Two Bears to his feet and walked him down the hall to the storeroom. Maggie and Colville followed. Maggie opened a drawer in a cabinet just inside the kitchen and pulled out a double set of keys. She stepped in front of the procession, took a firm hold on the heavy lock, and stuck the two keys in. The lock clicked open with a sharp snap. Kelly just nodded.

"Sounds like you got yourself a fine lock there, Maggie. This ought to hold him just fine." He opened the door and pushed the man inside. "You keep your mouth shut until I get back and you might make it through this alive, Two Bears. I hope you don't get any fancy ideas about trying to escape, 'cause if you do get out and any of them boys find you before I do, you're a dead man, for certain."

"I don't aim to do anything foolish. I'll be here when you get back. But don't take too long; I'm awful hungry. I'm afraid I haven't had much to eat for several days."

Kelly said nothing as he closed and locked the door. He handed the keys to Maggie.

"I don't reckon you should let him talk you into openin' that door, not for any reason, ma'am, empty stomachs included. I don't trust his word for spit," said Kelly. He and Colville left together. Kelly headed for the jail, and Colville to his barbershop.

"Don't say nothin' to nobody about where we're holdin' the prisoner, Colville."

The barber nodded and hurried on his way. Kelly carried his Winchester carbine at his side, a round chambered as always. His eyes darted from side to side as he approached the jail, and seeing nothing out of the ordinary, he went inside. Constable Jackson was sitting up, arms crossed, and looking as sour as if he'd just eaten a lemon.

"Looks like you got a worry, Constable," said Kelly.

"Does this look like a hotel to you, Marshal? I've had enough hombres comin' and goin' all day to start chargin' a fee."

"What are you talkin' about?"

"First, some gunslick storms in here lookin' for the Indian. When I tell him he ain't here, why he thunders out the door like a bull on a tear. Then, that rattler Galt and his sidekick, Free, wake me up demandin' to see the prisoner, too. I had to send them all away grumblin' and cursin' somethin' awful." An evil smile crept across Jackson's face as he broke into a chuckle. "I loved every minute of it, too."

"What'd you tell 'em?"

"Nothin'. Said I had no idea what you'd done with that worthless critter, nor when you was plannin' on bringin' him back."

"Thanks. I have him in a secure place for now, but I've got to get rid of the threat to his life before I can take him to Cochise to see a judge."

"You be careful. None of them fellas seem to favor peaceable solutions, 'specially that Galt. He's a mean one, he is. Soon as shoot you as look at you, and preferably in the back."

"We've met before. Listen, if anything happens to me, go see Maggie. She'll have a present for you." With that, Kelly left the jail and started down the boardwalk for the saloon.

As he pushed through the bat-wing doors, he saw a large man fitting the description of Preacher Ben Cutter and two others he assumed must be the Bourbonette brothers. The three were huddled at a table, conversing about something that seemed to have one of the brothers pretty heated up. There was no sign of either Galt or Daniel Free. That worried him. Where could those two have slipped off to?

He strode up to the bar and asked the bartender for a beer. He dropped a coin on the bar and watched as it bounced and spun around in a wet spot, then came to stop in the middle of a puddle of foam. He sipped his beer, keeping his back to the tables. He'd seen the man Cutter before, somewhere, but he couldn't remember where. He hadn't come up against him; he'd remember a thing like that. Considering the man's supposed reputation, he was surprised that they had not crossed paths before now. He decided that now was as good a time as any to introduce himself, chop a little wood, see where the chips fell.

"Howdy, gents, name's Kelly, Piedmont Kelly. Any objections to my joining you?" His marshal's badge was in plain sight, leaving no doubt that his visit probably had to do with something official, either Albert's death or the shooting of Gold Pearson. Or both.

"Nope. You're more than welcome to join us, Marshal," said Cutter. He reached out a hand. They shook. Neither of the brothers extended any greeting. It was obvious there had been tension between them, and Kelly's interruption was particularly unwelcome.

Kelly pulled out a chair and sat. He leaned the carbine against the table.

"Thanks. I couldn't help but notice you, Mister Cutter, your reputation seems to follow you around. I was told you were in town. Have we met before?"

"No, sir, I don't believe I've ever had the pleasure. These two here are Jed and Jake Bourbonette. They're from up around the Daleville area. We're here to do a little huntin'," said Cutter, with a wry smile. "You the marshal here?"

"The town does fall within my territory, I reckon, but it's well served by the constable. His name's Jackson, and he runs a pretty tight ship, so I hear. No need for me to spend a lot of time here."

"So, why *are* you in Purdy, Marshal?" said Jake.

"Well, you see I'm kinda lookin' into the killin' of your brother, Albert, boys," he said, fixing a serious glance at Jed. "And I was wonderin' if that might not be the purpose of your visit as well."

Jed nervously began scooting the empty whiskey glass around in front of him. Kelly continued to push him.

"In fact, might that be the 'huntin' expedition' Mr. Cutter mentioned? You lookin' for whoever shot Albert? I know one of you was the one that shot Gold Pearson, and I was curious as to what set you on his trail. What was it that made you think he was one of them that did the shootin'? You *are* on a trail of revenge, aren't you?" Kelly looked straight at Jed.

Jed was clearly shaken by Kelly's questions and the rapid-fire manner in which they came. There could be no mistaking that the marshal knew what they were there for, and there wasn't any reason to lie about it. If they really thought they could ride into Purdy, locate any others who were involved in the crime, gun them down, and ride out like nothing had happened, well that plan was finished.

Noticing Jed's uneasiness at the marshal's comments, Cutter spoke up. "Now ain't that just like a lawman, curious as hell? Even if he don't have no idea what there is to be curious about. Ain't that right, Marshal?"

Kelly grinned and looked around to see where Galt and Free might be. When he didn't see them, a sudden thought crossed his mind. A frightening thought.

Chapter Twenty-five

W hen Colville returned to his barbershop, he found two men waiting for him: Galt and Daniel Free. It was quickly obvious they weren't waiting to get a shave and a trim. Free was looking at himself in the mirror, splashing rose water on his shoulder-length hair and trying to finger comb a manageable part down the middle. Galt was sitting in the barber chair Colville had bought in Kansas City and had shipped by train to Tombstone, then by wagon to Purdy. He had $225 invested in the nickel-plated chair with a red leather seat, and he didn't look happy to see Galt pushing back in it until it almost tipped over, with his dirty boots hiked up on the counter.

"Help you boys?" Colville said nervously as he removed his hat and hung it on a peg.

"Reckon you can at that, mister barber," sneered Galt. "We come to buy something."

"Well, I deal in haircuts, shaves, baths, and a patch-up for the occasional gunshot wound. Which is it you boys figure you need?"

"Why we're not here for none of those things, we're here to buy some information, and the price we're willin' to pay ought to please you," Galt said.

"And what would that price be?"

"Your life, sir, your life. You tell us what we want to know and you get to keep yours. If you don't, well let's just say there'll be another hole gettin' dug up on yonder buryin' hill."

The marshal had made it clear to Colville who and what Galt and Free would be looking for, and warned him to keep what he knew quiet. Galt watched Colville closely to see if his allegiance to the marshal would outweigh his desire to keep on breathing. And would he go out on a limb to save Two Bears? Colville began to sweat, and his hands trembled, a dead giveaway that he knew just what was being asked of him, even if he *was* reluctant to share that knowledge. Galt had him, and he knew it.

"I-uh, don't know what information it is you are talkin' about." He looked away, busying himself with straightening up the array of combs, brushes, and scissors.

"Sure you do, mister barber. You know we're here after that rotten snake Two Bears for gunnin' down Silver Pearson right in front of our eyes and runnin' off with some of our rightful property. Now tell us where he's being held, or so help me, you'll never see another sunset. And that's a promise."

Galt eased out of the chair, pulled his sidearm, and held it not two inches from Colville's nose, so the man could stare down the barrel of the .44 and see first-hand what his future held. Galt's tactics of intimidation were working on the frightened barber, as his hands began to shake so badly he had to slip them into his pockets to gain control of himself.

"I-I reckon I d-do have some idea of where the man m-might be. So, if you'd be so kind as t-to lower that piece, I'll, uh, take you where I, uh, think he is," he said.

His reticence was a clear indication that he was struggling with the prospect of betraying the marshal's trust. When Galt thumbed back the hammer, the decision was made for him.

"I'll, uh, just be a moment."

But Galt wasn't going to be put off by any delaying tactics. He jammed the gun in Colville's ribs and growled, "Your last chance to do the right thing is right now. No stalling, or else you're a dead man. Do you understand?"

Colville nodded and hurried out the door. He headed for Maggie's place instead of just telling them straight out where Kelly had stashed his prisoner. As they left the barbershop, he looked like a man who was about to get sick right there in the street.

"Looks like we're headin' for Maggie's boarding house. That where the rattler is staked out, Colville?" demanded Galt.

Colville choked back his own rising fear as he said, "Now look, Galt, you got to promise no harm will come to the lady."

"Barber, we didn't come here to do harm to any what ain't in on the conspiracy to do us out of our money."

"What's that mean?"

"You just chew on my words for a spell and figure their meanin' for yourself."

Colville *had* obviously figured what Galt had in mind by the expression on his face. The Pearson foreman would see both he and Maggie as part of the attempt to keep Two Bears out of their hands, and that wouldn't bode well for either his or Maggie's future. Perspiration flowed freely down Colville's forehead, revealing the fear that now had a firm grip on a man whose only part in the whole affair had been trying to do the right thing. Now he was in danger of losing his life over it. No way out of his predicament had presented itself, and time was running out as they neared the front steps to Maggie's boarding house. Then, as Galt looked away to check the street for anyone who might interrupt his intentions, Colville made a move. It was a courageous act, but, a foolhardy one, as he turned suddenly and grabbed Galt's gun in an attempt to wrench it from his hand.

Galt easily overpowered the weaker man, twisted his

hand around until the gun was pointing directly at Colville, and cocked the hammer. But at the last moment, Free grabbed Galt by the arm and said, "NO! The marshal will hear the gunshot and come runnin'. Our only chance is to get Two Bears out of here without gunplay so he can lead us to the cash."

Galt took his finger off the trigger, and, instead of shooting Colville, broke the barber's grip and swiftly brought the butt of the .44 down on his head. Colville crumpled to the ground with a bloody gash on the forehead. He lay unconscious in the dirt as Galt and Free forced their way through the front door of the boarding house.

"Oh, Maggie, we've come to see if you've got a spare room," hollered Free.

From the kitchen, Maggie rushed to the front hallway as she wiped her hands on her apron. When she saw who awaited her, she stopped dead still. Her eyes were wide and her lips began to tremble.

"Wh-what is it you want, gentlemen?"

"Why Miss Maggie, we come to relieve you of a troublesome package, one I'm sure you're eager to be shed of," said Galt, his mouth twisted into a sinister grin.

"Whatever are you talking about, Mister Galt? I swear I can't imagine. I have no packages."

"Two Bears. We want him out here right now or you'll get . . ."

Galt was halted in his threat by Daniel, who stepped

in front of him before he could again draw his gun, perhaps using it on Maggie as he had on Colville.

"Mister Galt here is in a bit of a hurry, Maggie. All we want is to get Two Bears out of here without any fuss. So, if you'd be so kind, where's the key to your storeroom? I've been eatin' here long enough to know that's the only place in town, other than the jail, that the marshal could have stuck him and felt like he couldn't escape," said Free.

Galt started to make a move when Maggie hadn't responded to his demand fast enough. Again, Daniel Free kept himself between the two, nudging Maggie lightly to fetch the key. She knew all too well she had little chance to either defend herself or escape. In a final act of acceptance, she sighed, then opened the drawer where the keys were kept and drew them out. She handed them to Daniel, who hurried to the storeroom door, fumbled momentarily with the heavy lock, then swung the door open to reveal their quarry huddled in the corner.

Two Bears had heard the entire conversation. He saw his fate on the faces of Galt and Free who stood glaring at him through the open door.

"Get out here, you low-down turncoat," growled Galt.

Two Bears obeyed. The look on his face said he knew his doom was sealed. These men carried the stench of death on them wherever they went. Now, they had dragged it into this peaceful home all because of him. His eyes burned with hatred for his captors as his lips pursed with resignation. He would be dead before sunset, of that there was little doubt.

Galt grabbed him by his collar and yanked him into the hallway, then pushed him forward toward the door. He pulled his gun and jammed it into Two Bears' ribs.

"You got two minutes to tell us where the money is. If you don't, I'll drill you where you stand," said Galt through clenched teeth.

"Th-the marshal has it. He took the box away from me and stuck it in his saddlebag. And I don't know where he's gone off to, I swear." Two Bears held his shackled hands in the air and shook his head.

Galt frowned at Free, his mouth twisted into a question about what to do next. Then it came to him. He'd trade the Indian, and maybe Maggie, too, for the money. The marshal wouldn't dare risk a gunfight in which a woman might end up wounded, or worse, dead.

Galt pushed his two hostages down the hallway, out the door, and onto the porch. He waved the gun around, motioning Maggie to come down the steps and out into the street, to assume a place in front of him and Free, right next to Two Bears. They stood there for a minute, Galt uneasy at not knowing where the marshal was, hoping he was as yet unaware of their grabbing his prisoner. He looked around, and seeing only a couple of horses tied to hitching rails, and some dogs sniffing around a wagon making a delivery to the butcher shop, he raised his .44 and fired off one round.

Galt's attempt to grab the town's attention worked. Within seconds, several people had rushed out of stores and homes all up and down the street. Even the constable hobbled out of his jailhouse bed and limped to the door to see what was going on.

"Hey, what's all the shooting about?" yelled Jackson.

"Nothin' you need to be concerned about, Constable. We're just lookin' for some missin' property. Unless you know where it is, I'd go back to bed if I was you," said Galt.

Jackson ducked back inside. He hobbled over to the gun rack, where he pulled a double-barrel shotgun, broke the breach, and inserted two shells that he'd taken from his desk drawer. He snapped the shotgun shut, then stumped back to the door. He stood unsteadily on the boardwalk, raised the shotgun, and shouted at Galt.

"I don't know what you're up to, Galt, but if you don't put that hogleg away and step back from my prisoner and Maggie, I'm goin' to blow you to kingdom come."

Galt turned slowly to the irate constable; his eyes narrowed to slits.

"You'll never get me without hittin' the woman, you old fool. Now put that away and git back inside."

A sneer crossed his lips, and he started to raise his six-shooter in Jackson's direction. But before he could get it in a position to fire, Marshal Kelly stepped through the swinging doors of the saloon, his Winchester pointing directly at Galt, cocked and ready.

"Puttin' that gun away sounds like a good idea, Galt. Besides, I'm the one with the information you want. Deal with me."

Galt swung around to Kelly. "All right with me, Marshal. Now, if you'll just hand over the money the half-breed took, I'll be happy to make you a fair trade—these two for what's mine."

"Just how do you figure anything in that box belongs to you? It's all stolen from folks who earned it with the sweat off their brow. You never did an honest day's work in your life. You're nothing but worthless scum," shouted Kelly. He stepped off the boardwalk and into the street, straight toward Galt.

Furious at Kelly's words, Galt pushed Two Bears aside and yanked his six-gun up, cocked it, and pulled off a shot. The hastily fired shot tore a chunk off the saloon's doorframe, missing Kelly by two feet. Kelly's shot had no such error in its trajectory. Galt was thrown to the ground by the blast, with a gaping wound in his right shoulder. He rolled about, groaning and whimpering in the dirt, his gun arm helplessly bent beneath him. Kelly walked to him, kicked the .44 aside, and asked Maggie to see how Colville was, all the time keeping the Winchester aimed at Free.

As Maggie helped him to a sitting position, Colville

began blinking his eyes and grumbling something about being a fool. Two Bears stood motionless, as Daniel Free held his hands in the air, making no move toward his own gun.

Chapter Twenty-six

Maggie's parlor had taken on the look of a hospital ward. She had scooted the rugs aside while Kelly and Free dragged Galt inside. Two Bears, who was still limping from his own wound, helped Colville along. Seth Bonner had run across the street to the boarding house after the gunfire had stopped, not wishing to miss a moment of whatever was happening. Maggie quickly enlisted him in tearing some cloth bandages and bringing hot water while she secured a needle and thread to stitch up Galt's wound after digging out the bullet. Her mouth curled up in a subtle smile as she took the long, thin knife from Bonner. To the casual observer, one would think she was taking some morbid pleasure in seeing the man who had threatened her life in such pain.

Galt began cursing and moaning about the agony he was in as soon as Maggie began the task of locating the bullet. The thought crossed Kelly's mind that she was taking her sweet time locating the slug, but he stood by patiently, allowing Maggie the time she needed to complete the task. When she finished digging out the hunk of lead, she stitched up the wound as deftly as one would sew a quilt. As one last tribute to her getting even with Galt, she poured some alcohol onto the wound. He screamed like a wounded catamount. Maggie smiled a motherly smile.

"He'll live. Don't know whether that's good news or not," she said, as she turned to Colville and began examining his forehead where Galt had cracked him with the butt of his gun.

Kelly leaned over the groaning Galt, "You hear that, Galt? You're gonna live. Must be getting' old. I was aimin' at your head."

Galt glared at the marshal as he tried to sit up. Free leaned over to give him a hand, but Galt slapped his hand away.

"Next time we meet, Marshal, I won't miss."

"Next time we meet, Galt, it will be as you are led to the gallows for murder."

"Yeah? And just who am I supposed to have killed?"

"Well, for starters, you tried to kill Two Bears and me. Would have too if you'd been just a little better shot. Then there's that man near Daleville you shot down after you robbed him and set his house and barn afire. I reckon there have been others. They'll come to light by the time your trial commences."

"I didn't shoot neither of you two, Free did. And as for some man near Daleville, I don't know what you're talkin' about. I . . ."

"Hold on, Galt. I didn't try to plug the marshal, and you damned well know it. You can't pin that on me. I might have winged the Indian, but that's all," said Free, breaking in on Galt's attempt to put it all on someone else. Two Bears glared at Free's admission that he'd been the one to knock him on his butt with a lucky rifle shot. Two Bears scowled as if he were looking for a way to even the score.

Galt, who had struggled to his feet, reached for the doorframe to steady himself. The marshal moved to him, took him by his good arm and steered him toward the front door.

"Reckon we've caused the lady enough trouble. You'll spend the rest of your time in jail, at least until a judge comes by. Come on, Free, you're goin' too."

Galt looked at Two Bears and mumbled something about all three of them sharing the only cell in town, and how he liked the idea. Kelly quickly realized that his prisoner wouldn't stand a chance if put in the same cell as the other two. He had to come up with another plan.

"Sorry, Galt, Two Bears is stayin' with me. Why he might even end up the chief witness against you at your trial. I expect what he can tell a jury will make the difference between you just goin' to prison or gettin' your neck stretched," said Kelly. He pushed Galt and Free ahead of him and out into the street, straight for the jail. Two Bears trailed along, still shackled, with Bonner holding a six-gun on him. Colville had stayed behind while Maggie continued to tend to his head wound.

As they opened the door to the constable's office and jail, Jackson groaned as he recognized the prospect of trying to take care of prisoners in his condition.

"Damn, Marshal, you ain't thinkin' of leavin' these two with me, are you? Why I can hardly get around, let alone play nursemaid to a couple of gunslingers."

"Sorry, Constable, but I don't have a choice. Maybe you can deputize a couple of the townsfolk to lend a hand. Bonner here seems capable."

"Hmmm. Well, I dunno. How about it, Seth? You up to becomin' a deputy?"

Seth Bonner scratched his head, and mumbled something about expecting to get paid for it, while Kelly locked Galt and Free in the cell in back. He hung the keys on a nail next to the constable's desk and led Two Bears to the door.

"I'll take care of this one, Constable Jackson. I'll be back soon to question these two. C'mon, Two Bears, you and I are goin' to find a nice, safe place for you to ponder what'll happen if you don't cooperate."

As they walked back toward Maggie's boarding house, Two Bears said, "Marshal, there ain't much to tell. I done said that before. Why'd you let on to them two that I knew things that would get them hanged or sent to Yuma?"

"It won't hurt them to worry a little about you testi-fyin' against them. Might even make them decide to make a deal and come clean themselves." Kelly grinned broadly at the thought of playing them off against each other. Criminals, no matter how tough they act, always seem to crumble when facing punishment, especially when talk of a rope comes up.

An itinerant peddler's wagon rattled down Purdy's one and only street, tinware and leather goods slapping and rattling at the sides of the old flat-bed that had been converted into a traveling home for the man hawking his wares across the southwest. A mongrel dog followed along, head hung low as if he were tracking his next meal, undistracted by horses or people as he passed. The peddler occasionally shouted, "Come to William's merchandise wagon. I make the deals no one else will."

A couple of locals, who had rushed outside the saloon when the shooting started, chuckled at the ped-dler as he passed. After watching the marshal marching three men down to the jail, they shuffled back inside to return to what they had been doing before the ruckus—drinking whiskey. As they loudly commented on the doings outside, making their opinions known as to what should happen to Galt and Free, the bartender grinned and continued to wash and dry glasses, stacking them behind the bar.

The two drifters became loud enough to finally attract the attention of Cutter and the two brothers. When the action was actually taking place, Jed and his brother had been concentrating too deeply on their next move with Cutter to have been cognizant of the goings-on outside. Cutter had been out back in the outhouse, missing the action entirely.

Jed got up from the table and sauntered over to listen more intently to what was being said. The din of several drunken voices, the clink of glasses, and the overwhelming stink of smoke and perspiration tended to require mentally closing off a man's surroundings if he hoped to maintain his sanity. Jed's interest had perked up when hanging was mentioned.

"Heard you fellas saw what was going' on out there. Did I hear you say the marshal shot a man?" said Jed. "I figured them shots were someone blowin' off steam."

"Yep. That's what happened all right. Fella with a scar was wavin' a gun around, threatenin' to shoot someone, and makin' noises about some money that was owed to him. Then he turned the gun on the marshal as he stepped outside. The lawman plugged the man, clean as drillin' a rattler," said one of the men.

"You say he shot a man with a scar. Was he a big man, wearin' a floppy-brimmed hat, and a set of red braces for his britches?"

"That's the one."

"And the other, what'd he look like?" asked Jed.

"Skinny cowboy. Nothin' unusual about him. Carried

a big Remington on his hip, but he didn't pull it. Rangy kinda fella with a long, drooping mustache, wearin' a bowler. Say, why do you want to know about them? They ain't friends of yours, are they?"

"Nope. Just curious, that's all. Thanks for the information," said Jed, as he turned and went back to his table. Cutter had just returned from his trip out to relieve himself, when Jed sat down with a thud and a big grin on his face.

"We shoulda gone outside when that commotion started. We missed *some* doin's. And, now, it appears we have a change of fortune, dear brother. I think Mister Cutter here may just be out of a job."

Cutter's expression turned from one of casual curiosity in all the goings-on to one of intense interest. His long face took on a dark, intense frown. The lines in his craggy face seemed to deepen as his eyes narrowed. He pushed his hat back on his head, sat up straight and leaned over the table, looking Jed squarely in the face. His right hand dropped into his lap.

"Just what are you tryin' to say, mister? I'm the one who says when my job is done."

"The way I see it, Mister Cutter, we hired you to locate and eliminate the other three men who had been seen at our brother's place. When we arrived here, we found out that some half-breed had already put one of them in his grave. The other two, it appears, have now been arrested by that marshal, and hauled off to jail. They stand a good chance of hangin', or at least spendin' a lot of years behind bars. So, by my figurin', your job has been done for you."

"All right, then hand me my other five hundred and I'll be on my way," said Cutter through gritted teeth. "And I wouldn't be thinkin' of tryin' to cheat ol' Cutter out of his due, bein' as how I 'spect you two'd like to keep on livin'."

"It's just a fact, Cutter. If there ain't no one left to shoot, then it's clear your job is over, and we don't owe you one more red cent."

"That's how you see it, huh? That go for the both of you?"

Jed looked at Jake who was sitting tensely with both hands wrapped around an empty beer glass. He was staring at the table in dead silence. His eyes never moved at Cutter's question. Finally after Jed punched him on the arm, Jake grunted something unintelligible.

"I didn't hear you, Jake. Are you with me on this, or not?"

"I-I reckon, uh, I'm with you."

Cutter jumped up from the table, knocking the chair over backwards with a clatter. He scooted his holster around to the front and rested his hand on the butt of his six-gun.

"Well, boys, I reckon the time has come for you to either come up with what's due me, or pull them hoglegs. Either way, someone is going to die here today. Who's it goin' to be?"

Chapter Twenty-seven

Kelly was pushing Two Bears to tell him everything he knew about the Pearson operation. But the Indian was reluctant to tell too much for fear of hanging himself. Kelly sensed this and decided the only way to get what he needed about who killed an innocent man was to make a deal, one which would keep Two Bears off the gallows, and maybe keep his time in Yuma to a minimum. Of course, even if he made the offer and the Indian accepted, any time spent in Yuma was akin to hell on earth. He could only hope Two Bears had little knowledge of the place, although it was hard to imagine anyone who hadn't heard horror stories of the punishments meted out to inmates who strayed even slightly over the line. The rules were strict, and the guards had a reputation for being particularly brutal.

"It's the truth, Marshal, there ain't much I can tell you."

"Okay, here's what I can do for you. I can tell the judge you were within your rights to shoot Barker, since he shot at you first. Self-defense. And, since I saw the exchange with Silver Pearson, he *did* shoot at you first. Self-defense, again. I may be stretchin' the truth here a mite, but if you give me what I need, I can cut your jail time to a minimum and no prospect of stretchin' a rope. The deal stands only if you give me information I can use in clearing up this man's murder."

Two Bears reached up with both hands and removed his hat. He scratched his head and scrunched up his mouth, struggling with whether he should spill what he knew or keep his mouth shut, risking the worst. He knew there was a chance the judge would hang him for Barker's killing if he didn't cooperate with the marshal. Finally, he sighed his resignation of the matter. His chest sank in defeat.

"All right. I'll tell you what I know. I'm puttin' my faith in you keepin' your word," he said.

"Start at the beginnin' then."

"Well, that ranch you're talkin' about was only the second or third raid I'd gone on with the outfit. We had ridden along the San Pedro for a day or two, lookin' for small ranches that had few hands and were too far outside of town for folks to hear any gunfire."

"I thought you said there wasn't any killin'."

Two Bears looked at the floor. "There was a time or

two when folks didn't believe what Gold was sayin' to them that they should give up their valuables or get themselves shot. He'd throw a bullet or two in the ground just as a warning that he meant business. But no killin'."

"All right, go on."

"Well, we come to this little spread where it looked like one man ran it almost by himself. We'd heard about him from some folks talkin' in town about how it was a real shame about this fella, but that hard times had befallen him and he couldn't afford but a couple of hands. Gold figured he'd be easy pickin's even if there probably wouldn't be a lot of cash, so we rode out there. He was a little feisty when faced with the loss of what cash he had, but he didn't carry no weapon, even though he had a shotgun leanin' next to the door as the boys rode up."

"What did they do when they saw him?"

"Well, one of the boys kicked the shotgun away, then the others commenced to goin' through the house to see what they could find. They turned up some money and Gold said it looked to be a measely amount, but I never saw it. All the time, I was watchin' the goings-on from atop a hill down river from the ranch. I had me a real good view of the whole countryside and was to fire a warning shot if I saw anyone comin'."

"So you weren't actually down at the ranch house?"

"No, sir. I was standin' guard up on that hill. Gold said I was bein' broke-in to the doin's of the gang and he didn't want me underfoot if somethin' went wrong before he got to know my ways."

"But you had a clear view of what was taking place?"

"It was real clear that day. A man could see for miles and still spot a coyote making his way through the cactus. And I sure woulda known if anybody shot that man. Well sir, when Gold and Galt come outta that house, the man was makin' a fuss, mostly I reckon 'cause he wasn't used to a bunch of owlhoots robbin' him an' all. The boys just got on their horses and they all rode away, south toward Daleville."

"Did you all ride into town?"

"Yeah, the next day. That night we camped by the river. Since we hadn't seen anyone on our trail, we figured he hadn't told the sheriff yet, so, like as not, there wasn't nobody after us. We just went into town to seek out a saloon."

"Uh-huh. Did any of the bunch start a fire in the house?"

"Nope. There weren't no smoke comin' from anything, not even the chimney. Too darned hot for a fire, anyway."

"Where did you join up with the others?"

"I stood my ground. They come to me. Took 'em a few minutes to get up to where I was staked out."

"Did you hit any other ranches on your way back?"

"Nope, not for a couple weeks."

Kelly sat back on the couch. Like much of Maggie's furniture, the couch and chairs were covered with cloth and stuffed with horsehair. Needlepoint designs had been worked into the fabric; little flowers and birds adorned each piece. He felt at home here, but also was cautious about getting dirt on anything, or scratching the floors with his boots. That made him uncomfortable. He wasn't used to being in such refined surroundings. His thoughts turned to things other than the Pearson gang. Clearly they were a dangerous lot, but were they killers of unarmed men? Two Bears' story seemed to hold together. He had no reason to lie, considering what was at stake. On the other hand, he could have been in the thick of things and actually been the one to pull the trigger on Albert Bourbonette. Kelly shook his head, not certain of which way to turn.

The front door slammed as Colville came in holding his head and muttering something about big doings about to happen at the saloon. He fell, exhausted, and groaning into a side chair. He held his forehead, which was still wrapped, in a white bandage. A small bloom of blood had seeped through the cloth.

"What doin's are you talking about?" said Kelly.

"That big fella, the gunman that came to town with them brothers, well he's makin' noises like he's bound to shoot one of them. Looks like they've had a fallin' out."

"Reckon I'd best have a look for myself. Thanks for comin' and tellin' me, Colville. I think you'd best go lie down for a spell. You don't look so good," said Kelly.

"Reckon I will at that." Colville slowly got to his feet and shuffled toward the door.

Kelly motioned for Two Bears to follow him as he departed the boarding house.

"When we get to the saloon, I want you outside, by the door, out of the way. I don't want you calling any attention to yourself. And before you ask, no, you can't have a drink. If you even try to take off, I'll shoot you on sight, is that clear?" Kelly said. Two Bears gave him a hangdog look.

"Clear as glass, Marshal. I don't need any more attention at the present, especially with me bound up like a Christmas goose and no gun." Two Bears followed close behind the marshal as they waited for a wagon to rattle by, then crossed the street and stepped up onto the plank walk. Kelly looped Two Bear's shackles through the back of a heavy bench, secured his prisoner, and looked in over the swinging doors before he entered. Sure enough, across the room, at a table near the rear, Cutter was standing up, hand on the butt of his pistol, and makin' noises like a wounded bear. Kelly waited for a few minutes to get the gist of what the disagreement was over.

It didn't take long for the marshal to make out that Cutter wanted to be paid for something and the brothers were holding out on him. It appeared to have something to do with the men he'd hauled down to the jail just a while before. He eased inside, cocked his rifle, and slipped along the bar to where there was a clear space between him and Cutter.

"Preacher Ben Cutter, I'm U. S. Marshal Piedmont

Kelly. Don't recall whether I properly introduced myself earlier. But now would be a good time to take your hand off the butt of that six-shooter and settle your differences peaceably."

Cutter swung around at the sound of his name. "Get the hell out of here, Marshal. This ain't none of your business. These boys has got to answer to me for trying to swindle me outta money I earned fair and square."

"Just what is it they owe you money for, Mister Cutter?" said Kelly, without raising his voice.

"For trackin' down them that shot their brother, that's what. Now that they're in jail, these scalawags say they don't owe me any more."

"What were you supposed to do when you found these men?"

Cutter's eyes burned with rage. He showed no patience with palavering with this upstart marshal with the Cavalry Stetson and a Winchester. By his expression, he clearly didn't cotton to men interfering with his business, under any circumstances, and this one seemed determined to do just that.

Cutter turned to Kelly, briefly taking his hand off his Colt, exercising his fingers, then gripped his pistol again. His darkly steady stare made it clear he was intent on swatting this pesky intruder, and the sooner the better.

"Ain't none of your concern, Lawman. Now you can leave the way you came in, or figure a way to get that

Winchester up, a round chambered, aimed in my direction, and pull the trigger before I plug you. Your choice. But don't take too long. I got business with these two wearisome varmints."

Kelly didn't say a thing. He stood his ground, waiting for Cutter to make his move. Cutter began to sweat as he mulled over his situation. This lawman apparently hadn't heard of his reputation for being a killer with a fast gun. Hadn't Kelly heard about the ten men he was credited with killing? Or had he? Did he know of the real Preacher Ben Cutter? The man with a phony reputation? The man who had only killed one man, and that had been a drunk who had trouble getting his gun out of his holster?

Cutter's hand shook as he wrestled with the position in which he now found himself, whether to draw or back down and show all those around him that he was a charlatan, a pretender, a man who talked a good fight, but who, when pushed by someone with real talent might fold his hand. Had his day finally come? Had he pushed his luck too far? This wiry marshal didn't seem to be the type to back off and let things be. He must know something. Why would he stand his ground unless he knew the real Ben Cutter? He was either a fool or he knew his opponent. Was Ben Cutter up to the task of finding out?

"Well, Mister Cutter, can we sit and talk this thing over, or are you going to draw that six-shooter?" Kelly said, with a casualness that rattled Cutter. He didn't like the idea of being made a fool of here in front of all these people.

His fingers tightened around the grip of his Colt. His thumb rested on the hammer. Suddenly, he knew he had no choice. He had ridden into a box canyon. There was no way out, at least not with his dignity and reputation intact. His destiny was about to be determined in the blink of an eye. He'd either walk out of there with a bigger reputation, and the money that he felt was owed him, or he'd be dead. It was that simple. Kill or be killed.

His gun had barely cleared leather before the roar of the Winchester filled the long, narrow room. Smoke filled the space between the marshal and the gunman. Cutter's gun went off harmlessly into the wooden floor, and he dropped to his knees with a look of disbelief, then fell on his face.

Kelly lowered his rifle, and shook his head.

Chapter Twenty-eight

As Kelly motioned for a couple of the men in the saloon to drag Cutter's body out of there, he asked the bartender to find the undertaker. He looked over briefly at the two brothers who sat motionless at their table, eyes wide with shock at what they'd just witnessed. Kelly walked outside to retrieve Two Bears from the bench. He hadn't been certain of what reaction the town might have had to the half-breed being in attendance when a man was shot down. He knew people have a tendency to see what they want to see, and tell the tale the way they want to tell it. Things can get twisted way out of shape by rumor and innuendo.

"Don't say a word until we get down to the jail. I want to talk to Galt," said Kelly, hurrying Two Bears along.

The Indian, himself, appeared to be surprised by the turn of events. He tried to roll the last few minutes over again in his mind. He'd snuck a peek in over the swinging doors. He'd seen it all. He felt certain that if Cutter had known what he knew, that Kelly had already cocked the hammer on the Winchester, he might not have been so hasty with his decision to draw on the marshal. He was also puzzled by how slow on the draw a man with Cutter's reputation had been.

"Just one question?" said Two Bears.

"What is it?"

"I ain't had anything to eat now for quite a spell, and I was wonderin' if we could stop for a bite."

With all that had happened during the past three days, Kelly had nearly forgotten that little item. And now that it had been brought up, again, he too could use some of Maggie's hot stew. He steered Two Bears across the street toward the boarding house.

"We'll see what Maggie can come up with."

As they stepped onto the porch, Maggie came out with a worried look on her face.

"My goodness gracious, you're alive. I was so concerned you were walking into a hornet's nest, what with that gunfighter over there. What happened?"

"The marshal shot his gizzard out, Ma'am," said Two Bears, almost boastfully. "Ain't no more gunfighter." Kelly gave him a frown.

"Mercy, me." She just shook her head and wiped at her brow with her apron.

"Maggie, I wonder if you could find something for a couple of hungry men. Nothin' special, just something to fill some empty spots," said Kelly.

"Come on in, boys. I surely can oblige. Just you sit yourselves down in the dining room and I'll have something on the table in no time. Lordy, I sure am grateful you were around when all this nonsense started, Marshal."

"I figure I may have been the cause of some of it," he said. She ignored his words and hustled through the curtained door to the kitchen.

Fifteen minutes later, Maggie returned with a spread that looked to Two Bears like a feast fit for a king. He dug in without so much as a howdy, wolfing down fried potatoes, beans, and fresh bread as fast as his manacled hands would let him.

After stuffing his mouth full of beans, and then slurping half a cup of coffee, Two Bears surprised Kelly with a question. "What was it you were aimin' to ask Galt?"

"I want to see if he will back up your story about the Bourbonette ranch raid. He may not want to admit his part, but he'll likely either deny there was any killin', or he'll try to pin it on someone else. Either way, I'll find out if there was a killin'."

"You just can't bring yourself to trust someone who's half Indian, can you?"

"That doesn't have anything to do with it. I can't say I trust you that well, no. But I don't intend to set you up for something you say you had nothing to do with. You have enough hanging over your head without me adding to it."

"So you're sayin' if Galt confirms what I said, you'll back me with the judge?"

"If I find out you're tellin' the truth, yes, I'll stand up for you as much as I can."

"Then let's get to talkin' to Galt. I'm ready." Two Bears stood up, tossed his napkin on his plate, and started for the door. Kelly nodded and followed him out. Maggie came into the dining room just as they were about to leave.

"All through, boys?"

"Yes, Maggie, and a fine meal it was, too. Thanks," said Kelly.

"That goes for me, too, ma'am. Mighty tasty. Much obliged," said Two Bears, holding his hat in front of him.

When they arrived at the jail, Constable Jackson was sitting at his desk, picking through a pile of papers as he fanned himself with his sweat-stained hat, his wounded leg propped up on a wooden box. Perspiration dripped off the end of his nose. The whole room was in disarray with clothing strewn about like a Chinese laundry. Papers and trays of half-eaten food littered the floor around the makeshift bed he'd been using.

Kelly looked around bemused by the constable's untidiness. Jackson's gloomy mood quickly surfaced.

"I know what you're thinkin', Marshal, but just you

try to run a jail while you're hobblin' around like a three-legged jackrabbit. And them two you brought in ain't helpin' the situation any, either. Every whipstitch, they gotta be fed, or taken out to relieve themselves. When you gonna take 'em outta here?"

"They aren't goin' anywhere until the next time a judge comes through. In the meantime, I want to talk to them."

"Go on back. Tell Bonner he can rest a spell, or get himself a drink."

Kelly went back to where the prisoners were being kept. Seth Bonner stood up from his chair in the corner. He had a double-barrel shotgun across his lap.

"You come to spell me, Marshal?" said Bonner.

"For a few minutes. Stretch your legs. I'll let you know when I need you back here."

Bonner shot through the door in a hurry, wasting no time in getting free of his guard duties, and heading straight for the outhouse. Two Bears followed Kelly inside.

"What the hell's he doin' here? Get that skunk outta my sight!" yelled Galt, seeing his former compadre, shackled, but free to walk around. He rushed to the bars, reaching through in an attempt to get at Two Bears. "He ought to be in here instead of us."

"That's what we're here to talk about, Galt. I want to hear what you've got to say about a raid on a ranch up the San Pedro about a year back, where you and three others robbed a man, and shot him to death." Kelly watched carefully the expressions of the two men in the cell. Would their eyes give them away? Could either of them even understand the truth?

"What're you talkin' about? We ain't never robbed *and* killed no man. That'd be a good way to get oneself hanged on the spot. Robbery is good for some time in the pokey if you're caught, but killin' gets you the rope."

"Do you deny raiding a ranch near Daleville about a year ago? There was a man there by himself, remember?"

Galt sighed and hung his head. "Well, you got me there, Marshal. I reckon we did steal from him, but I swear we didn't harm a hair on his head. That's the gospel truth."

"So, when you left, what was he doin'?"

Galt nearly choked on the question. He began hemming and hawing like a man caught with his britches down in church. He looked over to Free, then scanned the floor for several seconds before he answered.

"Truth is, Marshal, when we rode up to the ranch house, you could tell he was a little fidgety when he saw us. He was was standin' outside with a double-barrel leanin' next to the door. I kicked the shotgun away, and Free held a gun on him while me and the boys took to givin' the place a good look-see for whatever we could find. I admit, we took all the cash and jewelry we could find. But I swear by my sainted mother, we didn't do nothin' to that fella." Galt was perspiring. His hardened, weathered face looked more like a whipped dog than a grizzled cowboy.

Kelly could see that Galt was most likely telling the truth. Daniel Free's nodding agreement spoke clearly as to the truth of Galt's words, too. The marshal was satisfied that Two Bears had been telling the truth, since all three seemed to have told of the same sequence of events. But now he was faced with a mystery. Somebody had shot Albert Bourbonette, but who? And how could he ever hope to find the man who did it? He got up and turned to leave, a puzzled look on his face.

"Hey, Marshal, what'd that snake you got trussed up like a hog to roast tell you? Did he say we killed someone? If I ever get outta here, so help me I'll wring your scrawny neck, you lousy breed, for lyin' 'bout me."

"Actually, Galt, you have him to thank that I'm not going to have you tried for murder. He backed up your story." Kelly gave a little salute and left the room.

Jackson was still trying to clean up some of the mess.

"What'd you get out of them two? Anything useful?" he said.

"Yes and no. It looks like they didn't have anything to do with Albert Bourbonette's murder. The fact that you found his watch in Gold Pearson's possession doesn't appear to mean much. Two Bears says he got it as part of a poker pot, anyway."

"So, does that mean those two back there aren't wanted for anything?"

"As far as I'm concerned, they're guilty of shooting

me and Two Bears. We both got wounds to prove it. They can sit there awhile. Maybe it'll change their outlook on life."

Kelly leaned against the doorframe and gazed at some of the people traipsing up and down the street, looking in store windows, and carrying purchases out to wagons or buggies. A woman coming out of a dress shop bumped into a gruff looking cowboy as she came out of a store. Her packages scattered all over the plank walk. The cowboy removed his hat, pardoned himself, and began picking them up for her. Kelly thought, *Now, that cowboy sure didn't look the type to have good manners. But then, things aren't always as they seem.*

That's when it hit him. While the stories told by Galt, Two Bears, and Daniel Free seemed to fit together like a hand in a glove, there was something out of place. Something he'd not considered, but now became all too obvious.

"Two Bears, you said the man was alive when you left and none of the gang set the place afire. That right?"

"Yessir. We didn't do none of them things."

"If Albert Bourbonette was killed later, then it had to have happened after you left, by someone possibly also looking for money. Did anyone look in any of the other buildings—the barn, shed, outhouse—to make sure there weren't any of the ranch hands still around?"

"Not that I saw. You can ask Galt, I reckon, since he was there."

Kelly did just that. When he reappeared in the office,

he had the answer he needed. No one had looked any-where but in the ranch house. The killer could have been there all along. He was the one that set the fire. But why? He told Jackson he would be back later as he and Two Bears closed the door behind them.

"Where we headed, now, Marshal?" said Two Bears.

"The telegraph office."

The two of them crossed the street to a small wooden building that sat apart from the other line of various-sized, false-fronted structures that formed the main street business district. When they entered, a bell tinkled at the door's opening. A small, pale-skinned man sat hunched over a clacking device, writing something down furiously. When the noise of the instrument ceased, he looked up.

Kelly had already drawn a piece of paper from a stack on a counter and was writing something down. When he was finished, he handed it to the telegrapher.

"I'd like this sent to the sheriff at Daleville, pronto. Mark it urgent. I need an answer as soon as possible. You'll find me at Maggie's boarding house when the answer comes."

"I'll send 'er right away." The telegrapher turned to the machine and began tapping out the message. Two Bears stood mesmerized by the man making tapping noises on a couple of pieces of metal, sending a message that would be received a hundred miles away.

Kelly had to pull him out of the office.

Chapter Twenty-nine

Kelly and Two Bears were sitting on Maggie's front porch later that evening when the telegrapher came rushing down the street, waving a piece of paper and calling the marshal's name. He ran up to the railing where Kelly was sitting.

"Here is your answer, Marshal," said the telegrapher, panting from his short run in the still heat of the late afternoon. Kelly thanked him and unfolded the paper. An understanding smile crawled across his sun-chapped lips.

"This just may clear up a lot of things, Two Bears. You said you were present at the card game where Gold won the pot that included the gold watch a gambler had tossed in. Would you recognize him if you saw him again?"

"I think so. It was smoky and I'd had a beer, but he looked different from the other gamblers that come around a saloon lookin' to make a killing."

"Where did this card game take place?"

"Up in Daleville. At the, uh, Gold Claim. It was when we went into town the next day after we had robbed that ranch."

Kelly drew himself up, stretched and said they were going to take a little walk. Two Bears looked apprehensive, but followed the marshal out the door anyway. The Indian exhibited disdain for his new role as pet dog to a marshal. Having to spend all his time with his hands clamped together in iron shackles was demeaning, and getting dragged along everywhere this marshal wanted to go was wearing on his nerves. If there was any way he could get free, he'd be gone without hesitation. But, of course, freeing himself while in the marshal's company was a nearly impossible task. He knew it, and he knew the marshal would never trust him by himself long enough to figure a way out of this situation. He might as well be in jail, he thought. At least then he could nap as he pleased, have someone bring him food three times a day, and not be constantly answering questions.

"Where are we goin' this time, Marshal?" said Two Bears.

"To see a gambler about a pocket watch."

"What gambler? And how would he know about any watch?"

"The one sittin' over in the Sure Shot Saloon. The one who just might be the one who lost it in the first place. If that's true, he might also be the one who killed Albert Bourbonette. That's what I hope to find out."

"Who is this gambler you speak of?"

"The dead man's brother."

As Marshal Kelly and Two Bears entered the saloon, they spotted the Bourbonette brothers at a table near the back where they had moved to withdraw themselves from as much attention as they could after the shooting of their partner. Kelly turned to Two Bears and spoke to him in a very low voice.

"I'm going to take a chance on you. Put your arms out and let me remove those shackles. Don't get any ideas about taking off; ideas like that can get a man shot. Understand?"

"Yessir. Thanks. You can trust me."

After removing the cuffs from the Two Bear's wrists, Kelly moved toward the table where the brothers sat. He hooked a chair with his foot and pulled it out, motioning for Two Bears to sit beside him.

"Hope you boys don't mind a little company."

"Why, uh, no, not at all, Marshal," said Jake. "Won't you have a drink with us?"

"Not at the moment, Thanks."

"I'd be glad to oblige, mister," said Two Bears. "A whiskey would go down real good."

As Jed started to raise his hand to summon the bartender, Kelly interrupted.

"My friend is joking. He doesn't drink." Two Bears frowned, leaned on the table with both elbows, and gave a huge, defeated sigh.

"Thanks for stepping in when Cutter got a little out of hand. I think he'd have shot both of us if you hadn't plugged him. We're in your debt," said Jed.

"He didn't give me much choice in the matter, did he? Seemed determined to get someone killed, even if it was him. He had an option to sit back down and talk it out. I'm sorry he made the one he did. A man shouldn't have to die just to save face."

"You're right, of course, but Cutter seemed to be a man who had to be the ramrod of the outfit. Nothing less would do."

"There are a lot of men out there who look at life that way," said Kelly. He leaned forward, looking Jed straight in the eye. His expression was one of serious contemplation, all business, light conversation now a thing of the past, although he said nothing.

"Was there something else you wanted to talk to us about, Marshal?" said Jed.

"Matter of fact, that's just what I wanted to do, ask you boys a couple of questions about your brother, Albert."

"Albert?" said Jake, a puzzled look on his face.

Kelly reached into his vest pocket and pulled out

Albert's gold watch and chain, laying them in the center of the table.

"Yep, Albert, and this here gold watch. What do you know two about it?"

Jed grabbed it up. He turned it over in his hand. There, on the back was the artful engraving that bore his name: *Albert J. Bourbonette, 1872, Arizona Territory.* Jed read the inscription aloud, then his expression turned dour as if he had been stricken with some awful memory.

"Where'd you come by this, Marshal? My brother Albert wouldn't have given it up except at gunpoint. It was a gift from our father."

"I thought maybe you could tell me, Jed."

"I-I wouldn't have any idea. Musta been those men who killed him and took it off his body. Was it one of those two varmints you got holed-up down at the jail?"

"No. It was found on Gold Pearson's body after you shot him."

"You mean he had it on him all the time?"

"Yep. Musta had it for a year or so."

"Well, I'll be. Reckon that puts the seal to it. Oughta be all the proof you need that he murdered Albert, ain't it? How else could he have come into possession of this watch?" said Jed.

"There is one little boulder in the path. Two Bears here says Gold Pearson was gambling with a man in Daleville the day *after* your brother was killed. He says the man was losing and offered to put this watch in the pot instead of cash. Gold agreed, and then won the hand, the pot, and the watch. Makes me think the man who lost the watch was probably the one who shot Albert, not Gold Pearson."

Jed stiffened at the thinly veiled accusation that he, a known gambler, had been the man at the table that night with the losing hand. Jake was frowning and staring hard at the drink in his hand.

"Sounds like you're accusin' me of somethin' I didn't do, Marshal. That what you're aimin' at? Puttin' me out front of a stampede? Why, I was down in New Orleans when it all came down. Ask anyone," Jed whined.

Kelly reached into his vest pocket and pulled out a slip of paper that had been delivered to him by the telegraph operator. He unfolded it and, as he started to read what was written there, Two Bears nudged his arm and leaned over to whisper something in his ear.

"He ain't the one, Marshal," he said, "It was . . ."

"I know, Two Bears, it wasn't Jed here who lost the watch. It was Jake. Isn't that right, Jake?"

At first, both brothers looked dumbfounded at such an accusation. Then a troubled scowl came over Jed as he spun his head around at his brother, and terror began to wrinkle Jake's brow.

"When your brother, Jed, came back to town after being gone almost a year, you, Jake, saw it as a perfect opportunity to rope your brother into helping you eliminate the one man who could identify you as the one who last had your brother's watch in his possession.

"And, after the Pearson bunch robbed your brother, the only thing left of any value was his watch, which you took off him after you shot him down. Your anger at Albert for failing to defend himself against the gang of thieves overcame your judgment. You not only murdered your own brother, but you burned every building to the ground, your way of diminishing him even further, I suspect."

Angrily, Jake finally spoke up, slapping his hand on the table.

"Some of the money taken was mine. I didn't trust banks much, either. So I left a goodly amount with him for safe keeping until I needed it. Business hadn't been good and the bank wanted to call my loan, so I rode out that day to retrieve some of my cash. Those men rode in while I was in the barn. Then it was gone, all of it, every damned penny, stolen by those four cowardly skunks at the point of a gun. And that fool Albert hadn't even tried to stop them," said Jake, his hand shaking, tears forming on his cheeks. "The bank was threatening me. Don't you see I had no choice?"

"Makes a man wonder why you didn't lend a hand at stopping the robbery, since you were so close. And if some of the money was yours, as you claim, you had a stake in keeping it safe," said Kelly.

"It was four against one. I'm no gunfighter. I—"

"How the hell could you have done such a thing,

Jake? He was our brother," shouted Jed, his eyes glaring at Jake. His hand moved toward his revolver, but he changed his mind when he saw the marshal watching every movement very closely. Kelly gave a subtle shake of his head. Jed turned and looked away in disgust, as if he could never again recognize Jake as his brother.

"But once Gold Pearson was dead, and could no longer identify you as the one who lost the watch, why did you keep up the search for the others?" said Kelly.

"I'd read about robberies of small ranches all up and down the San Pedro, and I figured it might be the same men. If I could locate them, I hoped to maybe get back some of the money they'd stolen. When Jed came back, I figured to get his help."

"But I'm bettin' you never told your brother that you were usin' him."

Jake hung his head. Jed looked away with the look of a puppy who had just been kicked. At that point, there wasn't anything Kelly could do to ease his pain.

"Jake, I'm going to have to take you back to Daleville for a jury to decide what happens to you. Stand up and drop your gun belt." Kelly snapped the shackles on Jake's wrists and began to push him toward the door. Before they had gone more than a few feet, Jed spoke up.

"Marshal, what was on that piece of paper you had there, anyway?"

"It was a telegraph message from the sheriff in

Daleville. He said Jake was gambling at the saloon the night after the raid on your brother's ranch. He said he had no idea the watch that was lost to a pair of aces belonged to anyone other than Jake."

"I just can't believe all this. My own brother near slipped a noose around my neck. It could just as easily have been me that got hanged if I'd plugged some innocent man. It's a good thing that Gold Pearson drew on me first, ain't it?"

"Reckon so." Kelly turned to Two Bears and told him to run down to the corral and get their horses for the ride to Daleville. The half-breed nearly knocked the door off its hinges as he made for the street.

With Jake in tow, Kelly stopped at the jail to tell the constable what had happened, that he was leaving, and that the lawman could do whatever he wanted to with Galt and Daniel Free.

"What about Two Bears? You weren't aimin' to leave him here with me were you? 'Cause if you were, I just saw him on that pony of his ridin' hell bent for leather. Why, he lit a shuck for the southwest like his tail was afire."

Kelly just grinned. "Imagine that," he said as he moseyed over to the corral to get his black gelding saddled, and find Jake's mount. Jed tagged along half-heartedly as if he didn't want to be associated with his brother. They had a long ride ahead.

Kelly looked over his shoulder at Constable Jackson. "I have a feeling you've seen the last of that troublesome Indian hereabouts." He gave the puzzled constable a salute, and whistled as he strode across the dusty street. From what he'd found in the Pearson's tin box and ledger, it looked like a few ranches along the San Pedro might soon be getting some of their losses returned.